Echoes of the Accursed

By

A. J. White

Contents

Author's Bio

Born and raised in the small, picturesque town of Pembroke, Ontario. Angela has always been surrounded by the beauty of nature, but it wasn't until life's chaos and the hustle of the city that her creativity truly flourished. A vivid imagination, nurtured form the events of the past, Angela would find her calm in penning down her thoughts. She has always dreamed big, that became her core inspiration in writing and creativity. Writing wasn't something she planned; it was something that came to her naturally. Her imagination, along with the books she devoured growing up, were the real spark. Being a young reader, she would aspire Christopher Pike as her favorite author, growing to read, thrillers by Stephen King, their storytelling resonates with her. While she loves to read good romantic comedy by Iris Morland or lighthearted read, she's drawn to darker stories, tales filled with mystery, suspense, tension, and emotional depth. That's where her writing tends to land: those in-between places where things aren't always what they seem, and secrets hide just beneath the surface.

Angela has spent her life mindfully, as she's an accomplished well-educated woman, she spent much of her time nurturing her three amazing sons, Cody, Brett, and Connor, dividing herself, being the fun hockey mom and the serious working mom. She is incredibly proud of what she does and indeed her versatility makes her stand out in the crowd.

The biggest pushes came from her family. Not only her children but her mother Judy, who has been her rock, her constant support system, always encouraging her to pursue what sets her soul on fire. She would like to express gratitude towards the other empowering women in her life, her aunts Bunny and Debbie, as well as Lorna and great friend Shannon, along with the rest of her amazing family and supporters.

Her only hope is that when readers finish one of her stories, they walk away thinking: *"That was a great read. I can't wait to read more."* Because, for her, storytelling is about connection—reaching someone in a moment, sparking something inside them, and leaving them wanting more.

I

She sat two feet from the gravestone marked with the name Philomena Burton. The damp night air chilled her to the bone, sending shivers down her back. Her quivering made the hairs on her arms stand on end...

Feeling the grave danger, "I don't want to do this," she whispered, pulling her hands away from the mucky soil, "my hands are sore," she moaned, stretching out her fingers and inspecting her nails.

"Then, use the damn garden spade instead of your delicate hands Harley!" Her friend, Tess, replied impatiently, rolling her eyes. "You know that's the best we could get; a shovel would have never made it through that tight ridged tunnel, so get over it!"

She shook her head and looked up. The black sky gave the moon an unnatural Amber glow, *like the whole universe seemed to know what they were about to do, and it was wrong.* "It's too quiet," she whispered. "Forgive me for this."

Tess smirked, "Speaking to the heavens again, Harley? What do you expect? It's supposed to be quiet; it's a graveyard!"

Brushing off Tess's sarcasm, she kept staring up at the starry night. The moon shimmered eerily like a spotlight, exposing their evil deed. "*Creepy,*" she thought, and shivering again from the dampness.

Looking back at Tess, she slowly mumbled, "I'm not sure about this anymore Tess, this is wrong. It's not a good idea, and I want to go home," she whined.

Tess slowly approached her and hissed, "If you want this to end, Harley, do it now!" Pushing her back down towards the grave, she warned, "*NOW, Harley, before the really bad shit starts*! Do It Now!"

She slumped to the ground and whimpered, "Stop shoving me. You know something, Tess? You can be a real bitch sometimes."

Tess, ignoring her comment, gave her another rough push.

"Okay, stop! Give me a minute to calm down. I can't stop shaking; besides we don`t even know if this is all true.

She trembled, the ground beneath her seemed to mock her hesitation. She swallowed hard, and reluctantly cast a glance at Tess. With a brief pause, she swept her dirty hands back through her hair, knowing she was unable to undo what was to surface.

"I don't...."

"*Oh, never mind*!" snapped Tess, cutting her off. "Let's get this over with, so we can get the hell outta here! I don't know what I was thinking, I should have known this would be too much for your weak constitution!" and then grinned with amusement, as she sat on the opposite gravestone, watching her slam the spade back into the ground.

From the sound of Tess's voice, she knew to stay quiet and not rile her friend any more than she already had, but it was too late. Her mouth shot back before she could stop it.

"You know, Tess, if you didn't take such an interest in my past, we wouldn't be sitting in this ghastly place full of decaying bodies."

Shocked by her sudden outburst, she lowered her head, digging harder, waiting for her friend to jump all over her comment before she could count to 3.

Yup, there she blows; she cringed as Tess shrieked back.

"Are you serious right now? Harley?" Tess asked, raising her voice, "Are you trying to blame me for all of this? Really?" She flung her arms up in the air, then marched over to her, pointing at a headstone in front of her, "look at that stone in front of you, Harley. Look! That is your grandmother, not mine! I'm just trying to help whom I thought was my best friend, so instead of being so whiney, you might wanna say *THANK YOU, TESS! I'm glad you came with me, Tess, you're the best Tess.*"

Her eyes widened; she could feel the rage build deep inside and clenched her jaw tightly. Holding back the angry words festering in her mind, *calm down*, she thought.

It's only one night in here, and I need her, but I will give her a piece of my mind later. Well, maybe, she mused, while letting out a slow breath...

"Remember something, Harley," Tess continued, then spat, sending a big gob at the ground next to her hand, hitting the side of her pinky. "Friends help each other. *So*, here I am, helping you. Be thankful, I didn't have to!"

"Okay, now that's just disgusting, Tess," she gagged, forgetting her anger. Pulling her hands away, she quickly wiped her defiled finger on her pants. God, will she ever grow up? Wondered as she threw sand over the rest of Tess's DNA.

Even though she was annoyed with her friend and completely grossed out by the spitball, she knew Tess was right.

This is all happening because of my own family, because of my damn ancestors and their inexplicable pull towards forces beyond our time.

The cold air seemed to tighten around her chest, but then something shifted. Her fingers, which had previously gripped the spade weakly, tightened. Noting Tess was unusually quiet, she turned and asked,

"What's wrong?"

Tess was staring at something in the distance.

Harley looked in the same direction, squinting through the foggy night air. *"Is someone coming?"* She whispered, her eyes straining to see.

When Tess didn't reply. She felt a bad energy pressing down on her from behind; the entire graveyard was suddenly cloaked in a creepy silence. She stopped digging, feeling the intensity of the moment. Her heart pounded heavily in her chest and breaths came in shallow gasps. After a few minutes she slammed the fork into the ground again, this time striking something with an unsettling thud. As she slid the garden spade, every scrape of the metal echoed through the silence while she waited for Tess to reply, amplifying her unease.

"It's nothing; I thought I heard someone," Tess finally whispered back, "it's nothing. I'm just tired."

But she couldn't shake the feeling Tess had seen something and wouldn't tell her. *Probably because she knows I'd lose my shit. And she was right.*

For the next bit, Harley focused on her digging until the muscles in her arms started to throb. Stopping for a minute, she wondered,

How the hell could Tess be tired, she's not doing anything.

Looking up at her friend, she cried.

"Tess, I can't do it anymore; I've had enough, I'm exhausted, my arms hurt, I'm choking on sand, and I'm thirsty."

Tess let out a dramatic sigh and passed her the water bottle, disregarding the rest of her complaints.

"You do know, your family was crazy to mingle in all of this. Who in the heck likes to explore Black magic? Oh yeah, *people who are in hell!"* She laughed.

Harley chugged the water back, not caring what her friend was ranting about. Tess's words were drowned out by each satisfying gulp she took. Looking at the bottle, smiling, she thought.

"Man, who would have thought I'd ever be this satisfied with water.

Finishing her last drop, Harley could hear her friend again and rolled her eyes.

"But, then again, maybe they aren't cursed, said Tess, "If your family was cursed, she continued , tapping her fingers on her chin, "*Ummm.*...truthfully, Harley, we really don't know, do we? I haven't noticed anything at all strange about you, like a long green pointy nose or something?"She laughed, mocking Harley.

Ignoring her childishness, Harley replied, "I'm being targeted because of a messed up curse, Tess. No one said my form was going to change."

"Well, we don't know enough about it to say for sure, do we? Except that you are the next generation, supposedly cursed, according to that letter we found left by your late Grandmother, umm, what was her name?"

 "It's Philomena," she snapped quickly, "I'm digging her grave up, for heaven's sake. Could you have at least some decencies and try to remember her name?"

 "Hey, can you try digging a little quicker? No, I take that back," whispered Tess tensely, "dig a lot quicker. So, we can vamoose. Let's forget about the letter for now," she murmured as she looked around. "I would help you, but we need eyes everywhere in this decrepit place." Tess looked back at Harley and threatened, "Better yet, I could always leave you right there, in that hole, in the dark, with the rotting flesh that festers below." feigning a ghostly voice, she moaned.

Harley's eyes grew big, "Tess, what's wrong with you! You wouldn't dare," she asked nervously as she started digging faster. "You can be so evil at times," she whispered, thinking Tess wouldn't hear her, but of course, she did.

"Okay, so I'm assuming you want to take your time digging and enjoy the thought of sleeping with the dead," she replied sarcastically.

When Harley looked up for a moment, she could see the sneer on Tess's face as she went on. Harley ignored her and started thinking back to the day they met.

It was when she was about 12, and her mom dropped her at the Roller DayZ Rink. Tess was standing with her roller skates hanging over her shoulder as Boy George was playing on the big screen during some Turtle race game. The goal was to roll around the rink as many times as possible until the whistle blew, and whoever went around most of the time won. People had to partner up for it, and she ended up pairing with a pushy, kind of take-charge girl, but she found her confidence was engaging,

"Hey," the girl said, as she walked up to her and dropped her skates "I'm Tess. Are you ready to take this rink over?"

"Hi, I'm Harley, and I'm not very good at this game."

"Oh, that's okay, Tess replied. You teamed with me, and I'm the best. People always lose when they play against me," she announced with a smile followed by a wink.

She thought she was about a year older than her. Tess spoke confidently and was somewhat friendly. She had a radiant smile, and her shoulder-length hair flowed a rich auburn. She had never idolized someone before meeting Tess, the perfect girl.

"As for you," Tess said with an imitating smirk, showing off her snow-white teeth.

"You just won't make a mistake,"

Then she told her to get on the wooden game seat, which was shaped like a turtle, or maybe it was an oversized bicycle seat; regardless, it was set up with tiny handles on each side and three wheels underneath. Tess did most of the work; she was quick on her feet while yelling out orders, as she pushed her around the rink. Thinking back, Harley acknowledged,

"Funny thing," she still orders me around.

Harley smiled as she shook her head. But overall, it was a lot of fun back then, and as for the race, Tess was correct; they did win, but it was 2nd place, not 1st. We did some sort of happy dance at the end. As for the reward, it was ice cream and fries from the canteen, and that's when they exchanged phone numbers, and they had pretty much become inseparable since then. She chuckled, thinking back to how excited they both were at that age over simple, silly games.

"HELLO," Tess yelled, "*you think this is funny?*"

Harley quickly snapped out of her childhood thoughts and disregarded Tess's remark. Instead, she was about to start digging again. But just as her hands started to plunge back into the soil, she froze as a low blood-curdling cry off in the distance cut through the dark. Tess jerked her head towards the sound; Harley immediately stood up in the shallow grave, straining to see what it was. Hardly breathing, her heart was beating wildly against her rib cage, so loud she was sure Tess could hear it.

"What the hell was that," Harley whispered, "I told you this wasn't a good idea... and I'm sure I just peed myself," she cried, trying not to think who or *what was in the graveyard with them.*

"Oh, stop being such a baby, probably just an animal of some sort," Tess mumbled quietly, her eyes still combing through the dark mist.

She noted Tess's fear as her confidence started to waver.

"Well, I hope it's only a damn dog or something small because we'd never survive anything big like a bear! Oh, and by the way, Tess, *animals don't laugh,*" she whispered, her eyes darting around as she slowly lowered herself back into the partially dug grave.

"Seriously, a bear? Come on, Harley! It's a graveyard filled with dead people in the middle of the city, far away from wildlife. Stop being melodramatic." Tess muttered, trying to steady her voice.

Again, they heard echoes of a cry, slowly shifting to an eerie chuckle, almost taunting them. Suddenly, the wind started to pick up, moving the night mist slowly, casting eerie shadows on the gravestones.

Quickly, Tess reached down and grabbed Harley's arm in a panic and tried to pull her up but couldn't get her to move.

Harley winched in pain.

"Ow!" She cried, and applied pressure to her arm, refusing to move, "why did you do that?"

Ignoring her, Tess leaned down and grabbed her shoulders, shaking her violently.

"Snap out of it Harley! *Get the hell up,"* she shouted frantically, *"hurry,"* pulling at her to climb.

Finally, her focus returned, and she realized what Tess was trying to do.

"Okay, okay, let go of my arm!" She blinked, shaking herself out of her frozen grip.

Tess quickly released her, terrified she turned to her with a look she had never seen before.

Tess was not one to be spooked easily, whatever she saw must have been pure horror, she thought, making her stomach churn. She tried to move, but couldn't, the fear was choking her.

Tess grabbed her again and tried to say something but was barely coherent. Taking a deep breath, she tried again. This time it was out loud and clear.

"RUN, Harley!"

Tess turned and started running, she tried to climb out of the grave, but everything was fuzzy. Falling back into the mucky dirt she tried again to get back up, and then heard it. The sinister laugh, louder and closer. Harley felt as if, whatever it was, was toying with her, calling to her.

Sitting quietly, fear gripped her as she shook uncontrollably, her heart beating wildly. Harley silently prayed it was her friend playing another one of her sick pranks. Strained and listening, there was only a dreadful silence again; even the wind was quiet. No branches moving, no muffled laughs, and what was worse, no Tess. Deep down, she knew Tess wouldn't take a joke this far, and as the fear rapidly engulfed her. Harley realized she was left alone to deal with whatever was out there, isolated, and feeling trapped.

Right then, a dark mist descended, giving her an overwhelming feeling of being watched, as an intense grip of evil filled the air around her grandmother's grave. Her gut feeling told her to get up off her knees and climb. Frantically, she gave herself a push, and now standing out of the half-dug hole, she steadied herself with her hand on the gravestone. Shivering, she looked around quickly, but all she could see were shadows moving in and out among some dimly lit stones. The clouds floated under the moon, casting a haunting fear that she couldn't shake. Her body trembling; she was struggling.

Pull yourself together, and move your stupid legs," but the fear was like a vice grip, and she couldn't move. Instead, she waited, hoping to hear Tess call out. She waited for what seemed forever. Nobody was coming. "Please talk to me Tess,*"* she mumbled, "just let me here your voice once and I promise to never complain again about your ignorant ramblings again."

She knew if Tess was there with her, she would at least know what to do. She was drowning in terror and couldn't yell out for fear of drawing whatever sick thing was out there toward her.

She sat for a moment with her head in her hands, twisting, then tugging hard at her hair, *I need to be strong,* she thought, imagining Tess bossing her, and with that thought, she jumped up, started jogging clumsily, slowly, and as her legs began to feel stronger, she started to run. It was so dark that all she could do was move with the shadows of the graves. Not knowing where she would end up, she kept running.

"Somewhere safe," she thought. Somewhere she could hide until daylight so that she could find her way out,"

As she tried swiftly moving between stones, the unleveled grounds made it more difficult; she couldn't see exactly where she was, and being blinded by the dark night made her sprint torturous.

Without warning, Tess disappeared. Just a few minutes ago, she was in the shallow grave just below her, Tess's crude jokes cutting through the cold night air. Then next, there was nothing but the oppressive stillness. She spun around, darkness blinding her, so much the graveyard was nothing but a hollow black hole, looming like silent sentinels.

"Where the hell are you, Tess?" She whispered, continuing to rage. "The friend that was supposedly so strong! I will never trust you again, wait until I get my hands on you, *"* she whispered growing angrier by the minute, *"How dare you leave me!"*

Harley mused, picturing Tess disappearing in the distance. she gave her head a shake, removing all thoughts of her, and slowed her run to a light jog. She looked behind, thinking she was far enough away from whatever that hellish screech belonged to, and that maybe she should rest. Instead, she pushed her aching body and decided to keep moving a bit longer. Trying to find the tunnel that she and Tess came in from.

But she suddenly stopped, reaching up; she grabbed her throat, feeling it closing in. Her legs felt like stone, and, at any minute, her body would drop. Not being able to take one more step, she landed on her butt and wrapped her arms around her knees. Terrified, she started gasping, trying to breathe slowly and deeply, realizing she was having one of her full-on panic attacks.

"Not *now!*" She moaned, trying to talk herself down.

"Breathe, just breathe, in and out, in and out."

After what seemed like forever, she finally steadied her breathing. Getting up slowly, she stopped, bent over, resting her hands on her knees; she felt a bit better.

Harley knew she needed to get out of there and slowly started running again. But the further she went, the panic seemed to grab her again. She felt as though she was being sucked into a black hole, moving deeper into the graveyard instead of towards the entrance. She felt like she was going in circles!

While battling her whereabouts, she stopped and let out a metallic scream, "Who are you? What do you want from me?" She waited, but the only sounds she heard were the rustling branches from the distant trees. Shaking her head, she muttered, I think I'm starting to lose my mind; I need to get out of this place," and started to run in another direction, only to trip, her hands trying desperately to break her fall as she hit the ground landing face-first into the dirt.

Dazed, she didn't move. Then, slowly, she lifted her head, groaning as she spit out soil. She moaned and gently rolled over. Intense pain made her cry out. Her hands and face started to throb. She touched her chin and felt the warm blood oozing from the fresh wound.

"Shit, what the hell was that?" Harley thought, as she looked around, but it was too dark to see anything. Slowly steadying herself on her knees, she started wiping the dirt from the front of her sweater and then moved her hand to her face.

"Ouch," she cried, as she dabbed her chin where it hurt the most. *"Damn, that hurts!"*

As she stood up, she bent over, shaking most of the dirt from her hair. Once she had inspected her cuts and scrapes and felt a bit settled, she started poking around at the ground to find what she tripped over. Dragging her feet slowly, Harley stopped once her foot made contact with something.

"What's *this*?" she wondered, crouching down. Her hand touched the surface of what she had tripped over. For a minute, she couldn't think, and then it hit her. The material was wet and felt cool; slowly, her fingertips tangled into a pile of wet hair. "*Tess, is this you? Quit fooling around*, she whispered frantically, "You're *freaking me out!*" she wasn't moving. "*Tess, please stop playing*," she whispered.

She abruptly pulled her hand away and wiped it on her sweater; she could smell blood, that unmistakable metallic smell. Harley started to feel sick as she crawled back and stood up. Shaking her head, she thought she was nuts, thinking she smelled blood.

"That's not Tess, that's blood from my own chin I smell; there's no way she'd do something so cruel. She can be mean, but she's not evil. And then she yelled so loud, her echoes bounced off every gravestone ahead, "Whoever is trying to scare me, get this, whatever is in my path, yeah, in my damn path, we will see who'll be scared once I find out who's behind this!"

Still not being able to see well, it dawned on her. "*Shit, I have my cell phone*," she whispered, unzipping her pouch with her trembling hands and grabbing it.

Holding the phone tightly, she thought again about Tess leaving her.

"I will never forgive you for leaving me behind, taking off the way you did. Ohhhh, you really have my back! Yeah right! BULLSHIT, Some friend! Thanks, friend! Paybacks are a bitch, and my friend, I will get you back." Harley mumbled angrily, turning on her phone.

Fearing the light on her cell would draw attention, she immediately pointed it towards the ground, but then she thought it best to scout the surroundings first. Besides, she knew her scream would have attracted the attention she so struggled to keep away.

Whatever is out there is probably on its way now. I have to be quick.

Her hand was slimy from whatever she touched during her agonizing stumble; fumbling with the phone, it started to slip; but thankfully, she managed to catch it with her other hand,

"Stop shaking, damn it," she muttered quietly as she tried to steady her hands.

Harley pointed the flashlight slowly ahead and then to both sides, making sure that nothing or nobody was watching her. Satisfied, she followed the beam along the ground in the direction where she had tripped. The bright light cut into the night, making her feel extremely vulnerable and nervous.

Shining the light ahead, Harley stopped dead as if hitting a brick wall. Her eyes took a second to comprehend what she was looking at...Falling to her knees, she started screaming, not caring about what or who could be lurking! Pure terror poured from her as she felt she was on the verge of madness. Slowly, the screams turned to sobs until her whole body felt like a dishrag.

"*TESS, oh my God, Tess. No, no, no.*" she cried, silently choking as her stomach heaved. Over and over, rocking back and forth in shock, unable to take her eyes off the grizzly scene.

Harley couldn't believe this was her Tess, who was sprawled out like a broken mannequin. Guiltily, she wished she hadn't seen her friend like this. The image of the horror of Tess lying on the ground, her head almost hacked completely off and twisted unnaturally. Her greyish-blue flesh looked unreal, like a cheap costume mask. She looked further up and gagged. Tess's eye was hanging out of her socket. Whimpering, she turned and pushed herself up. She would never be able to erase it from her mind. Weakly, Harley leaned on a nearby tree, moaning, and began throwing up.

She wiped the lingering vomit from her lips and spit, trying to remove the bitter taste from her mouth. Looking back at her friend's motionless body on the ground, her tears fell again.

"Tess," she whispered and then ran quickly, dropping next to her. She ripped her sweater off, softly covering her friend's head. Not wanting to leave Tess alone out in the cold, she had to move; shivering uncontrollably, she pushed herself up and whispered, sadly *"I'm so sorry, Tess, I never thought it would be this bad."*

Looking around to get her bearings, she read the name on the closest gravestone.

"Thomas Earle Perry," and then looked down at Tess again.

"As soon as I get outta here, Tess, I'll c...."

The screech cut through the night, making her freeze, and heart pounding in terror!

"Noooo, no more!" she cried, as she looked around, her eyes wide and wild. She yelled hysterically as she took off running the opposite direction of the sinister screams.

Running breathlessly, her throat was sore. Stopping to take deep inhales she bent over like a marathon runner taking in deep breaths. A stitch in her side, was now on fire..." *Great*, she thought, *I can't stand out in the open like this.*

She slowly walked, holding her side until she saw a huge dimly lit tombstone close by. Once there, she backed up against the large stone and slid down. Her mind was all over the place, especially Tess.

"She's *dead*," Harley thought, now shaking violently, *"Tess was dead."* Everything flooded her mind at once, and she was beginning to spin.

As she sat quietly in front of the stone, she felt something wet drip down her neck, creeped out; she jumped up, backing away from the tombstone, thinking a bird had pooped on the stone,

"Damn crows," she thought as she stood up.

The moon was hidden behind darkened clouds, making it impossible to see anything. She pulled out her phone again and shone the flashlight, her eyes growing as she read the sinister message,

DON'T TRY TO RUN! YOUR CURSE HAS JUST BEGUN!

Paralyzed with fear, Harley wiped her neck, which was still sticky and wet. She shone the flashlight on her hand, then back at the horrible message. Tremors violently streamed through her body when she suddenly realized the words were written in blood.

Harley knew she had to survive whatever was out there alone. She looked again at the message on the stone one last time. She could see the blood running down the center,

Oh my…, this was just written, she thought, *I had to be close when this happened.*

She vigorously shook her head back and forth, denial of the curse fading with each passing moment,

"It's true," she whispered, *"Tess was right; I inherited my ancestors' legacy."*

She started crying, tears running down her face, making little clean ruts along her dirty cheeks.

As she wiped them away, the rusty copper smell was unbearable, and she pulled her hand away quickly, using the backside of her jeans to remove some of the blood.

Harley's ears started ringing. Feeling dizzy for the 2nd time, her knees crumbled to the ground; she whispered,

"Nooo..." and her phone slid out of her hand, hitting the ground, the yellow beam of light resting hauntingly on the tombstone message.

She could feel the darkness coming over her as her eyes fluttered, she slumped sideways, lying silently in front of the bloody grave.

II

"Hey…, girl. Wake up!"

Before she could open her eyes, Harley felt pain all over her body, and let out a gasp as she tried to move. The continuous echoes deepened within her ears, as she slowly started to blink. Blinded by the sun, she attempted to clear the image of the person screaming at her.

"So loud," she cringed, cupping her ears for a minute and then rolled to her side.

She slowly pushed herself upright, against the stone. A shallow moan released from her lips as she painfully positioned herself. She looked back at the clean stone marked Joseph Crumble, confused, the threatening message was gone.

"What are you doing here? This graveyard isn't open yet. How'd you get through them locked gates?" the man asked, pointing somewhere.

Harley took hold of herself and quickly looked the old man up and down; his demeanor was unsettling. White tufts dotted his balding head, his face was pale and deeply wrinkled. He wore black scruffy work boots and blue ripped jeans; all were covered with patches of dirt and stains. She watched him as he wiped his grimy hands on his grey shirt, fitting snugly around his enormous waist, shivering at the sight of his black fingernails.

When the man leaned closer, she gagged from the lingering smell of sweat and booze. She grabbed her nose quickly; but the old guy didn't seem to care about her ignorant impulse. He just stared back at her with bloodshot eyes, looking somewhat sad.

A man with hidden secrets, she thought while studying him closely, noticing the sketched letters B.B on his top pocket.

"Hey," he yelled, interrupting her thoughts. "Are you listening to me? What are you doing inside the graveyard?"

Her head still pounding. Harley stared quietly for a moment wondering, before immediately snapping out of her gaze, and yelling.

"*TESS*!"

Her eyes widened as she sat up straighter, now more alert. Remembering she had passed out, not far from her friend's torn body. Harley quickly looked around, her heart racing, while she started clawing at the dirt. Still a bit disoriented, not being able to focus on the old man's interrogation, as she was to distracted by recent memories of her deceased friend's body, and the awful sour taste of residual vomit.

"Where is she?" Harley cried, panicking, as she looked up at the man still staring at her with confusion. Eyes blazing with fiery. "*Where is Tess*?" the anger in her voice was piercing, the rage she felt surprised even herself, and the keeper started to back away, almost tripping over his old worn-down shovel. "What did you do with her? You old fool."

"*Whoa!* Who is this Tess you keep talking about? He scowled back, immediately shocked by her accusations. "Just us here, girl. I`m just an old keeper, are you out of your mind or something?"

Harley watched him for a minute. The old man, still puzzled, scratched his head while mumbling something under his breath and then asked,

"What do you want here anyway, this early? And look what you're sitting on, girl;" pointing at the stone beneath her feet. "Get off and have some damn respect for the dead."

Harley ignored his remark.

"My best friend was with me, she was right here, and now she`s not," she sobbed, wiping the tears away with her filthy hands. "How is this possible?" She whispered, while crawling away from the stranger's grave.

The old man followed her, muttering more to himself, while she continued to move silently, fearing for her life. She suddenly stopped, kneeling on the grass between graves, she turned, looking up at him crying hard. And for the first time, she could see a hint of sympathy deep within his eyes.

The old man noticed the blood stain on her chin.

"What happened to you?" he asked.

But without a response she looked away. He leaned down, reaching for her, surprised, jerked back quickly before he could touch her,

"Come with me," the man said, attempting again, this time grabbing her arm firmly. "You need help. You're hurt."

"*NO!*" she yelled, "*you maniac!*" convinced he hurt Tess. She wiggled herself free from his grip, jumped up, and backed away, eyeing the shovel and then him. "It was you," pointing at the shovel. "You monster. You did this to her, where is my friend?" she accused.

His eyebrows merged and jaw clenched, as she repeated to yell accusations. More irritated now, he replied,

"Look, kid, I told you, I don't know what the hell you're talking about. I'm just a grounds keeper trying to help. Whatever happened here, leave me out of it. If you don't want my help, fine! I don't want part of any scheme's you kids pull on each other. It`s not my business but these grounds are, so get off 'em," he ordered, waving her away.

The man's face shifted from pale to a scorching red. She thought he might attack her at any moment. She stood firm glaring from a safe distance, ready for any swift movement he dared to make.

"Just get off the site," he ordered a second time, and turned his face to spit. "Have some respect for the dead woman that rests under your feet!"

She looked at the fresh dirt, wondering how he knew it was a woman. And as she glanced at the unmarked headstone, she thought,

"Could Tess be in there?"

At that moment, he leaned forward, reaching for his shovel, startling her. She jumped back, and then noticed something fall from his pocket.

Bravely stepping forward. Harley and the groundskeeper looked down at the object lying in the soil. Her chest feeling tight while watching the old guy pick it up.

"Here," he said, demeanor more relaxed, as he offered her the card.

She studied it for a moment without taking it. A tarot card with a picture of a man carrying a lantern in one hand, a dagger in the other.

Fear washed over her, she gulped, unable to speak, thinking about the chilling parallels.

A man on the card with a dagger, and a man in front of her with a shovel, right where she last saw her friends tampered body.

Is this card telling me he did something to Tess or was it just coincidence?

But as she tried to connect the dots, the old man interrupted.

"I found it lying on your chest when you were passed out. Drunk, I assume, but that's what you kids do these days. No discipline," he said, as he tossed the card to her, it landing on the ground again.

"I'm 19, old man. Do I look like a child to you?" she shot back, challenging him.

Ignoring her tone, he wiped the sweat from his forehead.

"I put the card in my pocket while trying to wake you."

Harley stared at the card lying in front of her, afraid to pick it up, the haunting resemblance still lingering in her mind.

"What?" he asked, grinning at her; "you scared of something? It's only a card, child," mimicking her.

"No," she snapped, and quickly grabbed the card from the ground. Looking one last time into his hollow eyes, she turned and ran away.

Seeking a place to hide, she eventually reached a tall monument to kneel behind, and catch her breath while she gathered her thoughts for a quick escape.

Tess and I came in from the south lot, Harley thought, as she started pivoting between the sites.

As she moved swiftly, her thoughts shifted to another family member.

You had to be buried in the biggest damn graveyard, Didn't you, Grandmother Burton!

Then her mind flipped to the chilling laugh she heard, right before she found Tess's body.

"Whatever that was, last night, may not be curable," she whispered, shivering so hard, not even the sweltering sun could warm her.

The idea of her friend being gone made her both sad and determined. She wiped a tear, looked down at the card, and clenched it tightly, whispering,

"*This curse or whatever it is, will end. I promise, Tess, and I will find your body, even if it kills me!*" and then slipped the card into her back pocket.

Peeking around another large monument, she saw the coast was clear and headed to a new spot, she peaked around the next grave site marked Billy Tash, the area still seemed clear.

Relieved, Harley took one last deep breath, and started her final sprint, eventually reaching the gate. Her heart leaped at the sight of her sage color jeep, the only vehicle in the parking lot.

She scanned the tall locked gate and then looked around for the tunnel opening her and Tess crawled though the night before. Not finding it, and thinking she might be trapped, Harley ran rapidly to the right, following the gate railings as they led to a flimsy fenced area.

 Spotting a gap near the ground, she attempted to pull the fence wider to slide though quickly.

The man yelled, startling her,

"*HEY!*, you can't do that!"

"Shoot, he must have followed me," she whispered, desperately squeezing through the narrow opening.

She ran to her vehicle, swiftly jumped in, and turned the key but it wouldn't start. Slamming her fists on the steering wheel, she screamed loud enough to shatter a windshield.

Now drained, wanting nothing but to give up, she remembered her promise to Tess, and quickly pulled herself together. Hoping for a miracle, Harley tried the ignition one more time.

"*Please, please, please,*" she repeated, holding her breath until the engine roared to life.

Eager to escape, she slammed the gas pedal, the car skidded, stirring up gravel, while it shifted side to side.

Harley cursed, before she gently pressing the brake with a shaky foot, and teasing the car into a forward motion.

Once in control, she whispered,

"I'm never going back there."

Knowing her statement probably wasn't true, she turned the radio up full blast.

The flow of reminiscing lyrics, blurred her vision, reminding her of precious years with Tess. Harley squinted her eyes tight, clearing her sight, as she wondered where she would be safe. Her friend Jordan came to mind. A slight burn radiated in the pit of her stomach, as she remembered the way Tess would treat Jordan.

Sweet innocent Jordan, she didn't deserve Tess's shrug-off attitude.

Feeling another pang in her gut, she immediately shook her head.

"What am I thinking," she whispered.

The guilt was eating at Harley, feeling as though she was backstabbing Tess. Instead, she focused on another individual, some might say, was the crutch between Harley and Tess—Enzo.

Caring and gorgeous, Enzo. Nicknamed the Spanish prince, she thought, involuntarily smiling.

Enzo was her best guy friend; meeting about a week after starting Vantage High.

"At least I would feel a bit safe with him, " she thought.

While contemplating between her two friends, a loud bang snapped her back to reality. Harley immediately pulled over to the side of the road, leaned her head back, and waited for her pounding heart to slow down before checking her side mirror. Seeing nothing, she turned off the engine to rest a bit longer, reluctant to leave her seat.

"Did I hit something?" She wondered. *What else could go wrong?*

Harley glanced in the rear view mirror, not seeing anything but her smudged reflection. Masked with dirt, forehead to neck, her eyes droopy, starving for sleep. Her chin marked by a cut, caked with crusty blood. Barely recognizing herself, she leaned closer to the mirror and noticed dried blood on her lip. As she licked her finger to rub the blood, she paused when her car suddenly darkened.

Thinking the clouds were covering the sun, she peeked out the window.

"Strange," she whispered, while squinting from the rays.

Confused, Harley relaxed back in her seat, leaning on the headrest. Wondering why the car was so dark, she continued to look around and then slowly merged her gaze with the mirror again. This time, her eyes widening, while her body stiffened.

A mysterious vale of dark grey mist, hovered over the back window.

Tightening her grip on the steering wheel, she quickly turned herself to look back and watched as a grotesque and malevolent face, emerged through. Its gnarl green nails, cutting against the glass, piecing her ears deep within.

Harley cupped them tightly, and turned away from the horror.

After some time, everything became quiet, and she looked back into the rear view mirror, squeezing her eyes shut and then opening them quickly, only to see something she wished she would not have.

 Red soulless eyes, staring back at her for only a second, before instantly vanishing into the mist, and then dissipated without a trace.

Trembling violently, she slowly adjusted her eyes on the empty road before her.

While gasping for air, she whispered,

"What the hell was that?"

Fearing for her life, she quickly started the car and sped away. Later pulling over, onto a side street, hoping to be far enough away from the evil entity, or whatever it was. Parking between vehicles, she shut the car off, and sat in silence.

Exhaustion weighing her down, she rested her head on the steering wheel, succumbing to the heaviness in her eyes, as she drifted into darkness once again.

III

Tap, Tap, Tap,

A sudden knock on the car window when she heard,

"Excuse me, miss, *HELLO!*"

Harley popped her head up quickly, confused for a minute, squinting from the bright sun.

"*Shit!*" she cussed, as she noticed the tall stocky man standing in uniform. Tensing up, she rolled her window down. "Oh, hi, officer. Is there a problem?" she asked, relaxing when she realized he was only doing parking enforcement.

"Yes, ma'am," he said, leaning in and removing his sunglasses.

Harley could tell he wanted a closer look at her face, but she quickly backed away.

"Are you alright, ma'am? Do you need some assistance?" the officer asked as he scoped out the inside of her car.

"No, sir, I'm fine."

"Miss!" the man says sternly, "You're in a time-limited parking zone, 2 hrs max. It's 8:30 a.m., and I've been on duty since 6, circling around here. You haven't moved your car. Are you sure you're alright?"

"Yes, I'm fine. I'm very sorry, officer. It was a long night at work; I pulled over and must have drifted off," she lied.

"Well, move your car, and let's avoid making this a recurring incident," he warned.

I have to get out of here, she thought, worried the enforcer would question her more.

"Go ahead, ma'am," he said, as if he had read her mind.

"Thank you very much, officer. It won't happen again, sir," and waved as she sped off.

The streets of Danvers, Massachusetts, usually brim with life, radiating a charm that often felt like the spirit of Christmas. Sidewalks bustling with the energy of people, while cars weave through traffic, honking and adding to the vibrant soundscape. Yet today, an eerie stillness enveloped the town, leaving her feeling unsettled.

As she turned onto Aliso Street towards Jordan's, she felt a mix of anticipation and nostalgia. She slowly pulled into the driveway, the engine running as she took a moment to soak in the beauty of the 18th-century-style home that sat before her—one of the oldest and most breathtaking residences on the block.

The striking red brick facade, complemented by pristine white shutters, created an inviting allure, while the rooftop resembled an enchanting old castle. A black iron-gated walkway meandered down the side of the house to the backyard, the heart of lively gatherings and cherished memories. Five graceful steps welcomed visitors up to a charming gray porch, where church-style doors framed large, dazzling diamond-shaped windows, inviting all who entered to experience the warmth and magic that lay within.

Just before exiting her seat, the house door flew open, and Jordan bolted towards the car.

"Harley! You're okay. I tried calling you back last night. I was worried after we spoke yesterday afternoon. You sounded really stressed," Jordan admitted before abruptly taking a step back, eyes wide. "What the hell happened to your face?" She asked.

Harley focused on Jordan for a moment, shifting back in her thoughts.

Growing up, they shared everything from clothes to secrets. But this secret may be too much for her. It may even scare Jordan away for good.

"Hello, I'm over here," Jorden said, waving her hand and knocking on the car to receive her much-needed attention.

Jordan was sweet and an amazing friend, but her attention-seeking nature could sometimes be annoying.

She was beautiful, a gem, so to speak; her outer layers sparkled. Her Spanish culture heightened her flawless skin, envied by most. Mid-length jet black hair with a natural wave that any girl would spend thousands to achieve. Jordan's innocence poured out through her warm hazel eyes.

Emerging from her thoughts, Harley replied,

"I'm exhausted, Jord. I will explain everything later. Right now, a hot bath and a bed would be great. I just need to close my eyes for a bit."

Without interrogating any longer, Jordan pointed to the house and said caringly,

"Okay then, let's get you settled."

"Can I park in the garage?" Harley asked. "I don't want anyone to know I'm here, thinking her hidden car would keep the malevolent being from finding her."

Not putting any thought into Harley's question,

"Sure, I'll get you settled, but you will explain later!" Jordan said firmly, staring her friend down, and she knew that look all too well. She was great at interrogating people.

Later that morning, she was awakened by a loud bang outside; jumping up quickly, she ran to the window, wondering what it was. The neighbor sighted her peaking out, dropped his tool and gave a wave, but she let the curtain fall without waving back,

"Beautiful home but creepy neighbors," Harley whispered.

She walked to a nearby mirror, and wiped the rest of the drool from her cheek.

"Ouch," she whimpered, as her chin started stinging when she patted it, a dreadful reminder of her trauma.

As Harley continued checking herself over, goosebumps chilled her. She thought about the malevolent thing she had seen hovering over her car window and sat back on the bed, as torture, and truth wrestled in her mind,

A maddening mystery of events that must be solved.

After learning about her family's dreadful mishap and discovering her friend's shattered body, she became convinced that it was real and needed to be put to rest once and for all. She felt a knot tighten in her stomach. Quickly, she pushed those haunting images aside and resolved to explain everything to Jordan as soon as she had her alone.

Struggling to get off the bed, Harley felt the pain radiate throughout her body and still couldn't understand why she was so sore. Wondering if something else had happened while she was blacked out.

Did that man in the graveyard do something to me while I was unconscious?

Overwhelmed, she rubbed her temples in an attempt to ease the throbbing pain.

She walked over to the closet and grabbed the towel hanging from the doorknob, and a warm smile crossed her face as she glanced around the familiar room, reflecting on her time spent in the house while growing up.

Sweet Miss Bozzelli, always treated me like a second daughter, especially after the passing of mom and dad leaving.

She loved staying at Jordan's house. She found life with her Aunt Winnie quite dull, as she didn't provide that motherly affection and traveled far too much for work.

She rolled her eyes, frowning as emotions began to overflow at the thought of her mom's hardships. Shrugging it off, not wanting to think about it anymore, she walked down the hall to the bathroom.

The air in the house smelled deliciously wild, filled with spiced aromas from the finest cooking. Sniffing deeply, stirred her inner child with comforting memories.

Jordan's mother was a great chef and owned one of the best French Restaurants in the City called La Bouche, despite her Spanish culture.

A perfect name for such mouth-watering aromas.

She dressed quickly after returning from the shower, throwing on light blue track pants with a white tank fitting snuggly under her hoodie.

Sitting on the armchair in the corner of the room, tying her white runners, Harley grinned at the sound of relaxing jazz music Jordan's mom loved to play while cooking.

"There," she said, standing up and glancing at herself in the long oval mirror.

Some of her friends would say she was gorgeous, carrying the look of a Hollywood movie star Marilyn Monroe, but they weren't convincing.

Harley let out an unsatisfied hum, tucked her wavy blonde hair behind her ear and shook her head while taking a closer look at her rosy, smooth complexion to make sure the makeup covered her wound completely.

"It will have to do," she said, and then left the room.

As she engaged the swirly wooden stairway, she could see it was beautifully decorated with white and coral satin bows while hues of mint sparkled at the seams.

She looked up at the antique chandelier; amazed how the peaked sun could beam through such a small window, creating a dazzling ray of warmth.

 Her face lit, enjoying the serene moment. But the pit of her stomach twisted again.

"Why am I feeling all cozy? I have no right to be happy after what happened to Tess, " she thought, as she approached the last step.

Harley could hear Jordan`s mom speaking over the music and let out a long sigh.

 Putting on a happy front, Harley walked into the kitchen.

That sweet smell of cinnamon, a typical, tasty Sunday morning breakfast at the Bozzelli's: delicious sizzling sausage, home fries, and savory French toast.

Harley rubbed her stomach.

"*Ah…*, refreshed and starving," she said entering, with a grin, while lying. "My stomach is growling Miss Bozzelli. Smells so good in here."

Jordan's mom greeted her with a tight hug,

"Where have you been hiding anyway?" she asked, as she set the plates on the table. "Sit, eat, and make sure to finish every bit. I cooked up a storm here especially for you, Harley. I know you're *famished*!" Jordan's mom said, smirking, while poking at her dramatic entrance.

"Thats so funny, Miss Bozzelli," Harley replied, forcing a playful ha-ha.

"Kidding with you girls is the highlight of my day," she said, chuckling. And I know how much you crave my cooking, Harley."

Jordan cut in with a squeaky laugh, "that's for sure," she said.

"And why are you laughing? My devilish daughter. We all know you can't get enough of my cooking either, always coming into the restaurant for free food."

Jordan's face grew red, "Mom, seriously, do you have to announce that to the whole world? Besides, it's so close to home; you made it very easy for me growing up, extremely accessible," she said with a smile,

"Oh, it`s my fault?" Miss. Bozzelli laughed, "And Harley, my sweet girl, how many times have I told you to call me Jan? Heck, call me Mom if you wish; anything is better than Miss." Jan said, scrunching her nose, looking more like Jordan's older sister than her mom. "You make me feel ancient. Besides, we consider you family in this house, which means a first-name basis."

Harley nodded and then scanned the generous amount of food stuffed on her plate while a wave of guilt washed over her, knowing all Jan's hard work would go to waste. She watched as Jan cleaned the counter, humming to a song, and her thoughts lingered as she took a bite of sausage.

How could Jordan's dad ever leave such a beautiful woman?

Jordan was devastated, and to this day, she still won't speak to him. A common pain she and Jord shared, the disappearing fathers, Harley thought."

After the divorce, Jan seemed to joke more than usual, but Jordan thought it was just her mom's way of covering up the pain.

Whatever the case, she was the strong, independent woman anyone would look up to.

Her married name was Andrews, and she could understand why Jan changed it back to Bozzelli shortly after the split.

Harley looked at her friend, and her heart sadly deepened. She couldn't count how many sleepovers she had, consoling Jordan when she woke up crying in the night.

"More juice, ladies?" Jan asked, pulling her from her sad mind.

Without a response, Jan filled their glasses, and set the jug in the center of the table before turning to walk away.

"Enjoy the rest of your breakfast, señoras. I'm off to my other home," she said, grabbing her Louis Vuitton bag from the counter and singing herself to the patio door. "Adios," and with a small wave, closed the door, leaving the room in silence.

As soon as Harley was sure Jan was gone, she shoved her plate aside, relieved she no longer had to force-feed herself.

From the other side of the table, Jordan, still filling her face, looked at Harley's plate and then her, raising her eyebrow.

"Are you feeling, okay?" Jordan asked, worried. "You're eating like a mouse; usually, you wolf mom's food down without a breath. Something's really off with you, Harley."

"What are you talking about?" Harley asked, her grin curling, and then aggressively shoved her plate under Jordan's nose.

Shocked by Harley's suddenly rude attitude, Jordan's face darkened in frustration, and she looked back down at her own plate. Harley quickly jumped up, leaning her face into Jordan's cheek. Jordan froze for a moment before slowly turning to her.

Now, nose to nose with her friend, Jordan could see a burning fire deep within Harley's eyes, a dark, wicked scowl, strong enough to torment a soul. Jordan gulped down the food in her mouth and leaned back just before she lashed out again.

"Harley grabbed and shoved the plate again. See, I've eaten some, JORDAN! I'm just not hungry, JORDAN! now emphasizing her name.

Eerie low cracklings echoed throughout the house, only Harley could hear. Jordan tensed more just before Harley smashed the plate on the floor, sending shards of glass flying everywhere.

Scared and confused by what she was witnessing, Jordan knew she had to do something. Breaking free from her frozen sitting position, she stood up and screamed,

"THAT'S ENOUGH, Harley!" and slammed her hand on the table.

Harley stared with a blank look, unresponsive to Jordan's voice. She grabbed a piece of glass from the table and squeezed hard, her jaw clenching through the pain as it punctured her skin.

Jordan instantly cupped her mouth, muffling her shriek, and clamped her eyes tightly, while her body trembled hard. Desperately pleading with her friend to stop.

Harley suddenly let go of the glass, and a small pool of blood followed. And as she became unsteady, Jordan ran to her, stopping her from hitting the floor. Grabbing her by the waist, she slowly lowered her down and then rushed to the sink to grab a towel. Still shaking, Jordan knelt beside Harley, gently lifting her hand from the floor.

After applying some pressure, she started dabbing it lightly while looking over the wound. Jordan was relieved to see that the injury was minor.

Harley started to open her eyes, moaning softly while Jordan rubbed her head.

"It's okay; you're okay now," Jordan whispered, fear still lingering. She hugged her friend tightly and helped her back to her feet.

Leaning on the backrest of the chair, her legs feeling week, Harley asked,

"What happened?"

"I have no idea," Jordan responded. "You went ballistic, scared the shit out of me, cut your hand and passed out. You tell me," her gaze hardening. "It was like something crawled inside you, Harley, something I never want to see again. You were unrecognizable."

Feeling numb, she could see Jordan's eyes were red and swollen.

"I don't know what came over me, Jord," she said, inspecting her burning cut. "I don't remember anything,"

Jordan leaned her hands on the table and took a deep breath, followed by a long sigh.

"I don't know what to say at this point," Jordan said concerned. "Until you open up and let me in. You really had me scared."

After listening to her friend's plea, Harley started cleaning the glass. A cutting quietness filled the room. Cautiously, she finished picking up all the broken bits and then shifted her focus to the blood-stain on the floor while Jordan filled the dishwasher. Soon after, both girls sat back at the table without a word.

Still thunderstruck, Jordan broke the silence.

"What if my mom were here?" Jordan asked, worried. "That was beyond insane, a freaking nightmare. In five minutes, your demeanor changed so fast." Jordan's words cut deep. "Seriously, what are you hiding? Spill your secrets!" her eyes narrowed, locking on Harley's tormented face.

Settling herself deeply in her seat, Harley hesitated.

"Ah, a question requiring an answer that will only scare you more, Jord," she whispered reluctantly, shaking her head. "I'm trying to keep you from harm. Please believe me when I say that." Harley took a deep breath and then spoke again, her voice low. "However, you do have the right to know, especially after what just happened."

"Okay, well, we have time now," Jordan said abruptly. "Spit it out."

"For starters, Jord, I have no concrete evidence." Harley said, "I have nothing to show you," and then paused momentarily.

Jordan sat patiently, staring. Harley could see the seriousness smudged across her pale-sweaty face.

"It's about Tess; the truth will be very hard to swallow. I considered telling you earlier Jord, but I didn't know how."

"Okay, and?" Jordan replied, impatiently, crossing her arms.

"Tess vanished."

Jordan rolled her eyes. "Is that all? You're joking, right? What do you mean, vanished? And what do you mean evidence? You're not making sense. She probably just ran off with some guy for a few days like she always has; it's her nature, that's far from alarming," Jordan said, shaking her head, not knowing the horror of that dreadful night.

Harley sat thinking for a minute, then sat forward, leaning her elbows on the table, cleared her throat, and then uncontrollably, the words flew from her mouth.

"Tess and I went to a graveyard, digging up a corpse because of an old family curse, and now, Tess is gone!" She slumped back in her seat.

Blinking rapidly, Jordan looked at her while nodding her head in a no motion. She cupped her mouth in disbelief.

"No way, you guys did not do that? *Gross*! However, I wouldn`t put it past you, Harley, since you always did enjoy trying to scare us with that imagination of yours, Jordan said, smirking. And as for Tess, she can't be too far; probably just freaked out; you must have pulled one good prank on her. She just ran off scared, as I would too, Jordan admitted, fidgeting in her seat." Have you lost your mind? Hanging out in graveyards." Disgusting.

Harley grabbed a pen from the table and started toying with it as she began explaining again, this time with clarity, recalling Jordan's earlier reactions

"Tess found a letter about a curse related to my ancestors. It gave us direction, and she was adamant to follow; I was reluctant. We went to my grandmother's gravesite. As I was digging, strange, creepy sounds echoed around us. We couldn't tell what they were or where they were coming from.

Tess, becoming nervous, said it was time to leave. She tried hard to pull me from the hole, but I was too weak to help."

 She rolled her sleeve to show Jordan the scratches as proof.

"After that, Tess ran, leaving me there alone. Once I regained my strength, I tried to find my way out, and that's when I tripped over something.

"Tess's lifeless body, just laying there." She said, saving Jordan from the gory details.

"And... then I passed out cold. But, when I woke, her body was gone, and some old keeper was standing over me."

Jordan pulled her hand away from her face, and jumped to her feet.

"She's just playing one of her sick jokes, right?" Jordan asked, "What have you done, Harley?"she yelled angrily. "Poor Tess, she's out there alone somewhere, scared."

"I knew it, Jordan. You're already being irrational," she yelled back, jumping up to meet her stance. "That's why I didn't want to say anything to you or the police. You already think I did something. I look guilty, don't I?"

Harley paced the floor, chewing her once dirty fingernails.

"I was the last person with Tess, the last one to see her alive and, what's worse, *dead.* Of course, you would think it was one of my pranks."

Harley sat back in the chair, crying, and dropped her head on the table.

Without consoling her friend, Jordan slowly sat down across the table and watched Harley in disbelief, with watery eyes.

Soon after, Harley raised her head and wiped her drenched cheeks.

"Please help me, Jord," Harley begged, "I don't think I imagined it, I'm sure I didn't, but nothing seems real anymore."

"What am I supposed to do?" Jordan asked, confused, not fully convinced Tess was dead.

"I expect you to Trust me! I didn't do anything to Tess; it was something malevolent!" Harley snapped, frustrated, that her friend didn't understand the depth of her horror, Harley slammed her fists on the table.

Jordan jerked back in her seat, nearly sliding off the edge, and swiftly grabbed the table to steady herself.

"*Not again!*" Jordan feared, drained from her last outburst, thinking she was about to unleash another raging episode. She shifted in her seat, preparing, just in case.

Harley could sense her tension.

"I'm fine," she reassured Jordan in a soft voice. "I'm just exhausted and frustrated. I can't shed those awful sounds from the graveyard, she said, keeping the gruesome images of Tess to herself. Truthfully, it feels like I just woke from one of my reoccurring, unwanted dreadful nightmares."

Jordan watched closely as her friend tangled her fingers into her hair and yanked. She leaned her hands on the table in front of Harley.

"Okay, stop," Jordan instructed firmly, trying to maintain her own composure. "Take a deep breath, release your hair, and put your hands gently on the table."

Jordan knew Harley had a nervous habit that caused her to pull or rip at her own hair when she became overly anxious in a quiet space. However, over the years, this habit had become less problematic as she replaced it with new techniques.

"Now, again," Jordan repeated, "breathe through the anxiety, and remember the exercises you learned."

Doing as she was taught; Harley took a few more deep breaths. Feeling her muscles relax, she slowly rested her hands on the table, watching Jordan's eyes follow.

"I'm terrified for you, Jordan," she admitted, her voice deeply concerned." I don't want the same thing to happen to you. I'm not trying to frighten you, but we can't ignore the possibility."

Jordan looked at Harley, her expression grim.

"Ha! That's an understatement. You already scared the heck out of me; besides, I'm a grown person, Harley. Now, please, just give me more time to think," she said, brushing her off and continued to rub her temples in silence.

She waited patiently until Jordan blurted…,

"*AND*, as you know, Harley, you do need me; you can't find Tess on your own." Tapping her finger on the table, she continued with a stern tone, "So, of course, I'm going to help you. I will be the one to decide my own fate."

IV

After a few more minutes, Jordan jumped up, leaving Harley sitting there. She ran and grabbed a rag from the sink and tossed it to her.

"Here, wipe that wound again while I grab some peroxide, and we'll wrap it up."

 As strong as Jordan was portraying, Harley knew her mind was quietly screaming and as she walked back into the kitchen, she started asking questions.

"How did all of this come about, anyway?

What was your family's connection?

There's more history, isn't there?

And what do you really think happened to Tess?"

The interrogation begins, Harley thought as Jordan began tending to her cut.

"As I said, it felt like a dream, Jord," she replied. "Only, it was real. The story of the family curse is real, something Tess discovered while snooping through the boxes in my basement after my parents... well, you know."

Harley squeezed her eyes shut and began.

"It started one day when I was gardening in my aunt's backyard, remember? I wanted to do that vegetarian diet and grow my own!"

"Yes, I remember," Jordan replied, eager to hear more.

"I asked Tess to go back to my parent's house and grab a specific garden tool, Aunt Winnie didn't have. Well, she was there for quite some time, nosing around. After Tess returned, she said, she spotted some old dusty bins in the basement while looking for the tool."

"Who does that?" Jordan asked, annoyed. "Root through other people's personal property?"

"Tess," Harley replied, abruptly. "It's what she did. She's always been nosey. I mean, she wouldn't be Tess if she hadn't."

"Well, you knew her better than I did, Harley, and you certainly had a lot of patience with her," Jordan admitted. "I was always the bystander when it came to you two. You must have noticed my lack of energy when she was around? I would always sit back and observe."

Harley looked down for a minute, "I know she didn't treat you the best, Jord, and I am really sorry about that. I should have spoken up."

"I'm over it," Jordan blurted out, shrugging her shoulders. "Don't grudge on it. I've learned to accept the way she was. Besides, I'll admit, we did a few *rare*, good times."

Harley shook her head. "You're a good person, Jord, and you're right; there's no need to dwell, so let me tell you more about the curse. Let me begin again. I sent Tess…,"

"Wait!" Jordan cut her off, holding up a finger. "Something tells me this will be a long story and probably creep me out some more."

Harley sat silently as Jordan walked to the pantry and searched for something. She returned with a bottle of Tequila.

"I think we need a strong drink, just to take the edge off, Jordan said, winking, "I don't know who needs it more, you or me."

Harley chugged back the rest of her juice from breakfast, making room for the liquor. She handed Jordan her glass, anxiously waiting for her to pore,

"Make mine a strong one Jord, I think I deserve it."

"Don't worry. I got you, Hermana," Jordan said amused, as she unsteadily poured two double shots into each glass.

 "Whoa, careful, Jord," she said, "All that clanging, and we'll be on glass cleanup again."

 "Sorry, I'm a little shaken from your maniac episode earlier, sister," Jordan replied, teasing. "Besides, that should be the least of your worries."

 Harley raised her glass, "clearly stated," agreeing with her friend.

Jordan shot her a playful look, scrunching her little nose while setting the bottle down gently, reminding Harley of Jan

The glasses clinked together as the two girls raised them.

"Bottoms up," they both said in unison, tapping their glasses on the counter before chugging their first drink.

They avoided discussing anything serious while they chugged a few back. The alcohol slid down easily, being their preferred drink since they were underage. For several minutes, they continued in silent agreement, matching each other shot for shot.

As soon as Jordan started feeling the effect of the Tequila, she broke the silence.

"This is so good," chasing her fourth shot with lemon and licking her lips.

Placing her glass on the counter, she directed Harley to the backyard, pointing to the patio doors,

"Let's get comfortable," she said, grabbing the Tequila. "I believe you know the way, *spice girl*," Jordan joked, winking at her as she swayed her hips amusingly, and lightning the mood.

Jordan will never let that night go. The most intoxicated, embarrassing nights of my life, performing on a stage, hypnotized by a magician, well, supposed to be.

We were about 16 at the time, sneaking alcohol before we went to some magic show. I, being all drunk and brave, ran up to the guy, trying to get him to pick me for one of his tricks. Poor guy, he honestly thought I was sober.

I soon learned it wasn't a trick I was helping with; instead, I was about to be hypnotized. Unfortunately, due to my poor state of intoxication, it wouldn't work. So, instead of letting him look foolish, I decided to stick around and pretend to dance and lip-sink a spice girl song; it was the worst night of my life, especially when I woke up the next day.

Harley jumped back to reality, "hey, that was a long time ago, Jord; besides, maybe one day he can hypnotize you to forget," she said, giggling.

Instantly stopping, Jordan looked at Harley and blurt out laughing, until they were grabbing their guts.

"Sorry, it was hilarious," Jordan admitted. You on a stage acting like the actual singer, and those hips," she laughed again, swaying.

"Okay, okay. I've had enough punishment. I think the tequila is making it a wee bit funnier," Harley announced, smirking, and reached for the door handle.

As Harley walked o the patio door, she realized the terrifying episode at breakfast was dissolving with every drink, and she liked it. Staggering to find her seat at the patio table, she took her hoodie off and sat down.

The weather was humid; a light breeze filled the backyard with a mild chlorine scent. Looking around the yard at the tall green shrubs, she took a deep breath, savoring the fresh air, and remembered helping Jordan decorate the patio area. Choosing seating sets, tables, and color schemes. The Pastel color of pale blue, combined with a deep sienna and terracotta, elevated its earthy ambiance, giving a vibe of 'feng shui.'

"Washroom break, before we're on pee clean up," Jordan shouted, laughing, as she rushed into the house.

A few minutes later, she returned with two glasses of chardonnay on a tray, along with some scattered fruits and cheese.

"Here, I brought something that will keep us hydrated and maybe sober us a bit," she said, chuckling.

 Harley cringed at the display.

"Not more food, Jordan. "I could barely stomach breakfast, but the thought was nice," she said, waving the tray away.

"Dehydration would be worse," Jordan argued, her words slightly slurred as she settled into the chair next to her. "I think the drinks are affecting us more than usual, and the heat will make it worse."

Jordan glanced up at the umbrella.

"Well at least we have that," she pointed out, and then pushed the tray closer to Harley, urging her to have some. "Go ahead and try a bit of the grape, anyway."

 Harley popped a grape into her mouth, as a means to please Jordan, and then asked,

"Alright, are you ready to hear about my family?

"Yep, let me have it," Jordan answered, raising her eye brows as she took a sip of wine.

She threw a final grape in her mouth, and just as she was about to speak, the side entrance gate flew open. Startling them. They quickly jumped to their feet staring.

"Hey, hey, hey, my beautiful Señoritas," Enzo said, with a grin as he walked by and jumped into the pool, water splashing on Jordan's light pink tank.

"ENZ," she yelled, glaring at him, her hand shading her eyes. My God! Could you make a more startling entrance," speaking dramatically.

"Ha-ha, sorry, Jord," his eyes lowered to her chest. "I see you bought a new bra," he said, joking, meeting her narrowed gaze.

The girls stood staring at him for a moment until Jordan look down, realizing what he was saying,

Eek! and she ran for the nearest towel.

"Not funny, Enzo," she said, annoyed, covering herself. "If I had known you were coming, I would have worn a swimsuit or locked the door. Next time, call ahead so I can lock you out."

Harley could see the pissed-off look on Jordan's face as she sat back in her chair.

Jordan turned to her and whispered,

"Remind me to move this table further from the pool. And we'll finish our discussion when our unexpected guest leaves," she said, pointing in Enzo's direction.

Harley smirked, "no problem," she replied, *saved by the handsome Spanish guy in the pool*, not wanting to discuss the evil family hex.

Both girls sat quietly, staring at the exchange student they met in high school; she remembered when she and Tess met him.

Charming, medium built, tanned skin, Dark silky hair, and piercing brown-eyed Enzo. "Oh, those eyes," she whispered, wonderstruck.

"What," Jordan asked.

"Huh, oh, nothing," she answered quickly, "I was just thinking out loud," hiding her true feelings for Enzo.

Harley and Tess fell hard for him, almost ruining their friendship until Jordan, their go-to counselor, jumped in. Poor Jordan. We must have put her through hell back then. Resolving most arguments with ease, and soon after, we realized that no guy was worth the trouble. Jordan never understood what they seen in him, as he wasn't even close to her ideal type.

"It's getting a bit chilly," Jordan said as she stood. Let's go sit over there," she pointed to a second patio near the outdoor fireplace.

Enzo climbed out of the pool, leaned over, and shook his head, removing excess water from his hair. Then, he jumped on one foot to clear his ear. Grabbing a towel from the lounge.

Harley almost drooled, checking out his wet chest, and anything else that could possibly be exposed, she smirked with a dirty mind.

"You girls, go ahead. I will meet you there with everything. Does your mom still keep the liquor in the same place"?" he asked Jordan, making himself right at home.

"Yes," she replied, irritated he'd be staying, "I think she and I had enough though, don't you think so, Harley?" putting her on the spot.

 She shrugged her shoulders, "Whatever, guys, I can take it or leave it."

Enzo jumped up.

"Then it's settled; another bottle of Chardonnay coming up," he yelled as he ran into the house.

Jordan smirked and rolled her eyes as she pointed toward the fireplace,

"Great, now he'll never leave," she said, "let's go get comfy again, I think it's going to be a long evening."

As they staggered over. The sun started to set, and long into the night sat around the fire telling their spooky stories, something they had done for years. She looked at them, thinking sadly,

The only one missing is Tess.

Not wanting to bring up the subject, Harley sipped some wine. The more she consumed, the less bothered she was. Feeling cozy, the gas fireplace did it`s best to keep them warm as the night air grew cooler.

"I'm still a little chilly, going to get my blankers," Jordon said, her words slightly sluurred. Otherwise, anyone?

"Come over here, I'll keep ya warm, Chica," Enzo said, smirking dirtily while patting the empty seat next to him.

"Annoyed anyone," Jordan answered, rolling her eyes and brushing off his flintiness. "No thanks. I'll be okay. I'll stay way over here in my own seat when I return. And, I trust Harley will be safe with you."

Just as she started to walk away, the flame spontaneously ignited higher, brightening the sky above them. They all jerked back. Harley was immediately alerted by a very light, sinister scream lingering around them as she watched Enzo jump onto his seat, holding his hands out as though he would karate chop someone. Jordon stumbled back, falling to the ground, her eyes fixed on Harley, who was still in her seat, hugging her legs to her chest. And then all went quiet.

After a few moments of silence, Enzo jumped from the chair, ran to Jordan, and helped her to her feet.

"Jeez, Jord, you should get that fixed," that shouldn't happen," he said.

Harley remained silent for a minute, gazing around in the dark yard, knowing it was something more. And then spoke up.

"Did you not hear that, Enzo," she asked, hesitantly.

"Hear what? Its fine, you guys," Enzo laughed, seeing the terror still etched on their faces. "It's just a short in the wiring or something. Have your mom look at it, Jord."

They ignored him until he started snapping his fingers at them, returning them from their trance. Harley was scared and wasn't shrugging this one off, she sobered up a bit.

"I hope your right, Enzo," Jordan said in a low tone.

"What else could it be?" he said, followed by an ethereal whisper, "the old wicked witch, ha," and then he nervously laughed as he ran his hand through his bangs. "You girls probably rigged the fireplace, playing a joke on me like Tess always does. Well, you won't scare me that easily, especially with this amount of booze in me."

"Yes, Enzo, we spent our whole day trying to devise some scare tactic. We revolve around you," Jordan said sarcastically. "You fool," she continued, "We didn't even know you were coming." Her brows narrowed, glaring at him.

Harley cut in. "Enough, it's like you said, Enzo, maybe the gas line," but wondered why they didn`t hear the scream.

Jordan shot her a look, confused, while her friend continued lying.

"It's just an issue with the fireplace, Enzo. Harley said. Jordan and I have no connection to any foolish jokes and I'm too exhausted to mess around.

Jordan stumbled to the chair for her sweater.

"Well, I need some sleep. Between the heat, the drinks, and whatever this was," swirling her finger towards the fire, "I'm starting to see double."

"Oh, come on, Jord, don't leave me alone with this hot Señorita," Enzo widened his smile at her, trying to lighten the mood. "I may not be able to control these hands," pretending to grope Harley.

Harley quickly slapped his arm, "Oh, shut it," she said. Giggling, unsure if her heated cheeks were from the drinks or his flirting. "I agree with Jordon; let's call it a night, I'll walk you out, big wolf," she said jokingly, pointing to the side entrance.

Enzo slumped with a frown, strolling to the entrance.

"Oh, cheer up, Enz," she patted him on the back. "Your poor dog look isn't going to help you this time."

He looked up, laughed, and said, "Adios, my sweet ladies," while dancing out the side entrance into the darkness.

She closed and locked the gate and returned to the table to start cleaning. Picking up the leftover tray of grapes, she asked.

"Hey Jord, do you still have that Old witchcraft book we used to look at?"

"Mom hated that thing. She lost her cool when she found it, remember?" Jordan replied. "She was supposed to throw it out, but I'll check downstairs. Why?"

"Just curious, I'm hoping for some answers. I still want to know about your family's past."

"Sure, Jord, but I need to see something before bed. Can you grab the book while I finish cleaning?"

"Yeah, no problem. "I'll go check now. But to be honest, I never really liked that book either. We should have burned it years ago with the Ouija board Tess left here, instead of just throwing the board away and keeping the book

Harley quietly cleared the counter without a reply as Jordan left for the basement. Before she brought the rest of the dirty dishes to the sink, she walked to the patio door to close and lock it, but as she approached, it slammed shut in her face.

She flew back landing on the floor. Grabbing her chest, she could feel the hard thump inside as she stared at the dark glass.

Fiery eyes pierced through; an eerie mist rattled the door violently as an ugly old face started to protrude. She backed away further, sliding herself until her backside hit the kitchen island. She sat frozen, pinned down, listening to the lingering scratches along the glass door.

Unable to scream or nudge another foot, Harley's heart raced uncontrollably until; the hold released her just when Jordan entered the room. She quickly turned away from the wretched evil, hiding her face in her hands.

"Here it is, Harley. You're lucky; Mom forgot to get rid of it. Don't let her catch you with it!" she warned, skimming the description on the back cover as she walked to the counter.

Harley gazed back at the glass quickly and caught only a glimpse of the end of a face receding back into the mist and instantly vanishing. She knew now, she wasn't imagining things.

The Old Hag was unleashed!

Jordan walked to the other side of the kitchen island, looked away from the book and stopped abruptly.

"What the heck are you doing on the floor?" looking down at her puzzled. "Here is your crafty book," she said.

Harley ignored it, jumped up and ran to the door, looking out and scanning the patio area.

The book slipped from Jordan's hands, falling to the floor, creating a loud bang that echoed through the kitchen.

Harley turned and screamed, triggering her friends scream. Jordan then jumped away from her, holding her arms out to shield herself.

"Wow, it was an accident," Harley, she said, trembling. Her face was stern. "You really need to chill. You totally freaked me out. It was only the book. Why are you so jumpy now? What happened this time? And why were you on the floor? You look like you saw the devil, my gosh."

"It's nothing," Harley said, shaking her head. "I think a bird hit the window," she lied. Not wanting to get into a full-blown conversation, "I'm just tired. Dishes are in the sink. I can do them in the morning if you want."

"You've had a lot of nothing happening lately Harley," Jordan said, sarcastically. "There's not a chance I'm accepting that, and there's no need to do dishes; Mom has the cleaning lady on Fridays, so don't worry about it. Let's get some sleep, and we can finish our conversation tomorrow."

As they started ascending the staircase, Jordon stopped Harley by grabbing her arm.

"Hey, do you think we'll find Tess?" She asked.

Harley stopped before answering, swallowed hard, and without looking back, she said, "I can't say Jord, but we will talk in the morning, okay? I promise," and continued up the roving staircase. "Goodnight."

When they got to the top landing, Jordan gave her a quick hug, "Goodnight," she said and turned toward her room at the other end of the hall.

When Harley entered her room, she closed the door, leaning on it with her back; she sighed deeply and looked down at the crimson book she held.

"Black magic craft," whispering the title. "Okay book, let's see what I can learn about disappearing friends and invisible attacks."

She took the book, sat on the bed, turned on the lamp, and began flipping through the pages. Coming across an interesting subtitle, she stopped,

"Beyond the Grave." *What's this about?* And began reading.

Conjured from beyond the grave, the spell that has been cast is among the most sinister. A person with genuine witch ancestry can be cursed if they attempt to reach out to an ancestor beyond the grave, thereby opening a portal. The evil crosses through during a red moon and will pursue a third generation in the family. "Hidden amongst the evilest Witches, lies...,

The Old Hag,

Harley threw the book on the bed.

"Is that what happened?" she wondered.

She slammed her fist on the bed angrily.

"It's all because of my family's past; there's no other reason. What doesn't make sense is the letter Tess found. It said, "The curse would begin on my 20th birthday, but I'm only 19. Also, this means the old keeper may not have hurt Tess, but why did Tess die?"

Harley was baffled. She lay back on the bed, thinking about the gravesite, knowing she had to return to finish what she and Tess had started. After reading the ancient letter, Tess believed it was true. She now wishes she had taken it more seriously.

"Damn your curiosity, Tess," Harley mumbled, her eyes filling up, "I should have left you behind. I would have, knowing the truth now."

A single tear ran from the corner of her eye, her body shivered for a minute, and then she slowly pulled the blankets over her head, rolled to her side, and drifted into a deep sleep, one she needed now more than ever.

V

A dark force held her back, preventing her from running ahead. She looked down at her feet; they were moving, but she wasn't getting anywhere. Despite her strongest efforts to push forward, every step felt impossible.

As she screamed in frustration and strained against whatever was holding her, a chilling laugh echoed from behind, intensifying her fear. Glancing back quickly, nothing was visible.

"Where are you? Come out and show yourself!"

The force that had paralyzed her, released her so suddenly that she fell to her knees. Immediately, she yelled,

"WHO ARE YOU?"

But this time, only a piercing squeal swept past her.

Quickly cupping her ears in pain, she scanned the drifting shadows. Pushing herself up, she noticed a flickering light in the distance. And unexpectantly, a strange energy settled upon her, filling her with strength and urging her to face her fears head-on.

Moving swiftly now, through the narrow path. Her intuition continued to scream,

"Run away Harley," but this time her body moved towards the cabin.

The deeper she floated into the dark, silent woods, the shadows sharpened, twisting around her like an octopus would drag its prey to the most bottomless black abyss.

The mystery of what lay ahead fueled her, and her voice echoed over the silence,

"I`M HERE IF YOU WANT ME, she yelled, awaiting a response in anticipation. "SHOW YOURSELF, WITCH."

As she moved closer to the light, the old rustic cabin stood about 10 feet ahead—a broken-down relic from the late 17th century.

An empty white chair creaked as it rocked back and forth, causing her muscles to tighten.

Looking up at the porch roof, she gasped as her eyes widened at dead rats, hung by their necks, their lifeless bodies dangling from the damp red ropes, swaying against each other inexplicably.

Her hand shot up to clamp her mouth as she stared at the grotesque scene.

"How are they smashing like that?" She whispered, observing the lack of wind.

Finally able to take a cautious step, she felt something nudge her from behind. Jumping, she turned swiftly, glancing in all directions, but nothing appeared. And then suddenly…

Something shoved her again, this time landing on the floor of the welted patio.

Letting out a low whimper. She looked ahead at the looming old walls; the brown logs that carried bits of black mildew between the cracks.

A dingy, green film, lightly coated the window to the right, leaving just enough light to see a strange eerie mist surrounding it, giving a haunting sense of familiarity.

Slowly backing away, fearing the fate that awaited her, her body trembled uncontrollably, heightened even more by the torturous smell of rotting meat, she grabbed and squeeze her nose.

Then instantly a strong gust of wind brushed by, and something scratched her arm, making her shriek loudly. Pushing herself to kneel, then stand, she used the decking to quickly regain her balance and stood silently for a minute, gripping her burning arm.

Hesitantly, she dared to move another inch, but implosively, she moved closer to the door.

Carefully stepping to the sides of each rotten board, the creaking with each step only increased the tension within, making the thump of her pulse stronger than ever.

Just as she took her final step, she was shocked by another attack, feeling a hard punch to her shoulder blade.

Flying forward, moaning, while pinned against the old scratched up door; something paralyzed her, pushing so hard that she gasped for a breath.

Feeling like this was the end, the suffocation so strong, her body shook violently until it finally let go.

With another loud gasp of air, she calmed down and took a few more deep breaths, feeling the tension release.

Looking down to a burning area of her leg, she could see her track pants soaked with blood, and a feeling of warmth flow to her ankle,

Pulling her pant leg up for a closer look; she wiped the minor scrape and took a breath.

Looking back at the door, she limped forward, and started to reach for the handle but stopped; instead, she grabbed her sweater from around her waist and put it on, cradling her fear and chill.

Not knowing what to expect on the other side. Slowly, reaching for the old rusty doorknob, she gently twisted it; a low grinding made her tense up and release it quickly, pulling away.

Giving her hand a vigorous shake, she grabbed it again, but as she tried to open the door, she heard another muffled scream coming through the window at the right. She let go of the knob quickly and turned, creeping toward the sound.

Approaching it quietly, she peaked in and could see a round pedestal table that looked of wood and iron, about 2 feet from the window.

As she continued to search through the dark film, gently wiping it for a better view, something landed on the top of her head, startling her. Pulling away quickly, she looked up only to see a dead white and red, rat, dangling above her.

She released an instant shriek and cupped her mouth again as the thick fluid started to run down the side of her cheek.

Pulling her sweater over her hand, she quickly wiped it away and returned to her brief investigation.

Something stood in the center of the table, surrounded by 13 geometrical shaped objects.

"What is that?" She wondered as her curiosity deepened.

Wanting a closer look, she walked back towards the door and grabbed the handle with more force this time, but just as she was about to turn it, the door flew open, sending her to her butt.

Grabbing her chest, she stayed there for a minute, expecting something to jump out at her, but nothing happened. She took a deep breath and jumped to her feet.

Now sweating with panic, she wiped her forehead, and then stepped into the dark house, hearing nothing but the thump echoing from her ribcage.

Walking in slowly, she whispered,

"Hello, anyone here?" and immediately covered her nose with her sleeve from the pungent odor.

As she moved swiftly around the room, her eyes landed on it: an old leather-bound journal lay wide open on a stand to the left of the table. She ran and grabbed it.

Weighing heavy in her hands, she observed it under the candlelight to see its edges frayed with age.

Is this what I am supposed to find?

 The cover was perfectly etched with a symbol she somehow felt connected to—an intricate, swirling knot, but she didn't understand its meaning, and under the knot read the word Runes.

Scanning more of the area, she could see a wooden object holding what looked like black crystal stones. Drawn to the items, she was lost in time, until suddenly, the candles flickered high above her, snapping her head back.

The light instantly revealed some writing etched into the wood, prompting her to lean closer again, and then out of no where...

BANG.

Jumping back, fearing as she turned to look.

The sight of dark silhouettes crawling up the walls, had had made her freeze and hold her breath until curiosity propelled her toward the shadowy noise, where she found herself staring at a small curved staircase nestled beside a large brick fireplace with flaming coals.

 Ignoring her twisting gut, she stepped slowly, creak by creak as she walked up the lonely dark stairwell, stopping half way to look back,

Feeling as though she was being followed, another twist in her stomach caused her to clutch it, and then vomit, coughing up a dark green fluid.

Realizing she was struck by another force, she threw up again, this time, losing her balance. She began to fall, plunging into darkness. Echoes of ghastly screams piercing her ears from every direction.

Fighting for her life, feeling the despair, she tilted her head back, allowing herself to descend deeper into the black void, resigning to her fate. The darkness and screams devouring her.

"Wake up, please, wake up," the words started to blast heavily in her ears.

Straining to open her eyes, she blinked several times. Feeling her body trembling as she heard the words again, this time loud and clear.

"Wake up, Harley."

It was Jordan.

"Jeez, are you feeling, okay?" Jordan asked. "What happened? I could hear you talking in your sleep, loud enough, that the creepy neighbors probably heard. When I ran over, your arms were raised as if you were fighting something off. It was freaky! When did this start?"

"I'm okay," she said, wiping the drool from her lip as she sat up. "Just one of my nightmares."

"Also," Jordan said, pointing to the floor, "I noticed something beside the bed."

She leaned over the edge to see what Jordan was pointing at. She saw a puddle of greenish liquid on the floor, swallowed hard, and shook her head in disgust.

"How the hell? I must have thrown up during the dream. It's gross. I'm so sorry, Jordan," Harley replied. "I'll clean it up."

"No worries, I hope you're feeling better; lucky you didn't choke. I think it's time to see a doctor, Harley."

She stood up slowly, still feeling a bit woozy. She swayed without Jordan noticing.

"I'll clean it and take a shower. I feel fine now, Jord," she lied, not wanting her friend to smother her.

Jordan walked out, leaving her rooting through her backpack for fresh clothes. But as she started for the shower, down the hall, Jordan peeked her head out of her room and stopped her.

"Hey, Harley."

"Yeah, Jord."

"What was it about, your dream?" Jordan asked.

"I'll tell you all about it as soon as I clean up," she lied.

As Harley continued for the washroom, Jordan asked another question, one she didn't want to answer.

"Hey, do you think we will find Tess?"

Harley buried her face into the rose-patterned towel,

"We need to discuss that in more detail too, Jord," she replied, "later okay."

"Okay, I`ll go make coffee. See you downstairs."

Harley turned on the shower and let it run for a few minutes to warm the water. Placing her towel and clothes on the counter, she undressed and tossed her soiled clothes into the hamper. After using the toilet, she approached the counter to grab a razor.

Just as she reached for it, something tightened around her hair and slammed her face against the mirror. She couldn't move her head; her lips felt tight. She quickly raised her hands to the glass and pushed back hard, frantically fighting to break free. In that moment, she heard a chilling whisper in her ear:

It's your turn, Harley," followed by a spine-chilling chuckle.

She could see a glimpse of something gruesome in the mirror; a dark hand with long, pointy, blood-covered fingernails, clamped down on her shoulder. She was able to focus her eyes down at the counter and spotted a razor blade; able to move only her hands, she grabbed it and, with one fast painful stroke, sliced through her skin.

As the warm blood trickled down, she thought,

It's not a dream.

Fearing what was yet to come. She heard the creepy voice again,

"*You're all mine soon.*"

Still fighting to break free, the malevolent hag continued to paralyze her.

Minutes passed, and with one last effort, she placed her hands back on the mirror, summoning all her strength to push herself away. As it released her, she flew back into the bathtub, her legs dangling over the edge.

"Leave me alone!" she cried, terrified, as she pulled the shower curtain closed for protection. "Who are you?" She demanded, but sat in dead silence.

A cold breeze swept over her feet while she peered through the gap of the curtain, which she clutched with her life, as she watched in horror. A dark gray mist slipped through the window, slamming it shut, making her jerk back in the tub.

Harley sat uncomfortably for a moment, cold and shivering, until she cautiously moved her shaky hand towards the swaying shower curtain and yanked it open, scanning the room. It was gone.

She felt her hand throbbing; the small gash was still bleeding. Jumping up and grabbing a facecloth from the hook, she wrapped it, her mind haunted by the whispered words.

This thing is tormenting me. It has the power to kill me, why does it keep me alive?

VI

Harley grabbed another cloth from the counter and washed quickly. Still shaken, she dashed down the stairs, the smell of coffee brewing in the kitchen as she approached. "Make mine a strong one, and then we need to get going," she told Jordan eagerly, keeping the washroom incident to herself for the time being.

"Where are we going?"

"I need to research something. I will explain once we get there," she replied.

Jordan approached the table where Harley sat, passed her coffee, and sipped on hers quietly, leaning against the island. She had questions, but dismissed the thought of asking.

"Where's your mom?" Harley asked.

"She went to the restaurant early. They have a big function today. Mom had to make sure everything was perfect, maybe investors," Jordan replied, as she placed her cup on the counter. "I don't always pay attention, but I should; I may be responsible for that place one day."

"Okay, let's go," Harley jumped up quickly, ignoring Jordan's last statement.

"Wow, what's the rush? I barely drank my coffee," Jordan asked, as she placed her cup down and grabbed her purse.

"It's important," Harley replied, without a full explanation.

"Fine," Jordan whined, rolling her eyes. "I'm right behind you."

While the girls headed for the front door, they heard a thump upstairs. Harley turned quickly,

"What was that?" she asked, startled.

Jordan also turned, listened for a moment, and said, "It's probably just the wind slamming one of the doors; however, after everything you went through, I can understand your jumpiness," and motioned Harley out the door, "Go ahead, I'll lock up."

Soon after, they pulled into a parking spot near the entrance of the Bayville Public Library.

"Jordan, have you ever heard of the Old Hag or runes?"

"What? No, why do you ask?"

Harley parked the car, turned off the ignition, and let out a long sigh. She explained her dream and how she found the runes book, and that they were essential for the symbolic ritual. She spoke of the family curse caused by a summoning, and reiterated that she needed to dig up an ancient grave to retrieve something from it.

Jordan looked at her as though she were losing her mind.

"You're not making sense," she said. "curses aren't real; they're just superstitions."

Harley paused for a moment before continuing, her voice steady.

"Tess uncovered something shocking: our family is under an ancient curse that targets third generation females, caused by a spell due to a summoning gone wrong. But here's the kicker—It's supposed to happen in the female's 20th year. I'm only 19. This all came about because Tess became suspicious while I was busy preparing the backyard garden at my aunt's house, as I mentioned yesterday… Remember?

"Yes", Jordan replied.

"During Tess's visit to my parents' partially empty house, she stumbled upon a mysterious box containing a letter about this curse. It revealed that I needed to visit the grave of the last ancestor who was killed, giving the name Philomena Burton, a grandmother I never knew I had, until that letter. I am supposed to retrieve something essential for a ritual. The letter was signed by someone named M. Burton, but I have no idea who that could be. That's all it said," she confessed, carefully holding back the whole truth before continuing.

"Tess also found disturbing information online about this kind of curse. It's tied to a dark force that has remained hidden, yet every few generations, women would vanish without a trace. To be honest, Jord, I didn't think I had any connection to this kind of stuff. I honestly laughed at Tess when she first brought it up, but you know how she reacts when people dismiss her concerns. Interestingly, my parents have never mentioned anything about this, leaving me with more questions than answers."

Jordan looked terrified and asked,

"Where is Tess, Harley? I still can't believe any of this to be true. It has to be some deranged lunatic, right? There is no such thing as a curse. Maybe your imagining things."

"Well... it gets worse," Harley started to confess, "Tess pushed to dig up my grandmother's grave to get what we needed. I didn't want to do it, but you know how she was, right? She wouldn't let up. Tess kept pleading, so I gave in, as morbid as it all sounds."

Jordan just sat there listening to her story, wide-eyed and speechless.

 Harley continued to tell her friend about how Tess was there one minute and gone the next. Harley told her she had seen Tess's dead, partially dismembered corpse, revealing all the gory details this time.

Jordan flung her hand to her mouth and gagged, leaning her head out the door quickly.

Harley jumped out of the driver's seat and ran around the car to help her friend, but the scene was too hard to stomach, so she moved to the back end of the vehicle to get away from the odor.

Having a sense of how Jordon felt, Harley worried,

"Are you going to be okay, Jord? I didn't want to tell you everything, but I needed you to believe me; I'm so sorry to put all of this on you."

Jordon heaved again,

"Yes, I'll be fine," she said, motioning Harley away and then spit.

After the reality became apparent, Jordan jumped out of the car, wiped her mouth, and stood momentarily staring at her friend.

"Did you go to the police?" she inquired.

"With what, Jordan?" Harley asked, frustrated. "No one else had seen Tess there but me, not even the groundskeeper, and no one believes in ancient curses. What do I tell them? Hell, it's my family burden, and I didn't believe it."

"Well, we have to find Tess; we have to do something about it, Harley," Jordan said, squinting her eyes devilishly.

Harley locked the car doors.

"That's what I am trying to do, starting here at the library. The dream I had when you woke me, made me think? Maybe these runes can help, and that old cabin has something to do with all of this; I need to research these things."

Harley could tell Jordan was still in shock, and leaned in to hug her.

"I don't know, this is all crazy, Harley," she sobbed. "I have known you for years, and nothing happened.

"That's the thing, Jord; it concerns my age, I think, however, I could be wrong. Anyway, Tess and I had been planning this for a few months; we didn't want to involve you because we know how fragile you are," Harley stated, "but weird things have been happening all around me, everywhere I go, the incident in your kitchen, and in the bathroom."

"Huh," pushing away from Harley's hug. "What incident in the bathroom?" Jordan asked.

"How about I save that for another time?" she answered, "You have heard more than anyone else could handle, plus we have a lot to do."

Harley grabbed the library door and mumbled as they entered, "If Mom were still alive, I would ask her, but truthfully, I don't think she knew much anyway; One thing I'm sure of is that I am being aggressively attacked, Jord."

As they walked in, Jordan stopped. "You mean what happened in my kitchen, When you went all crazy?"

"Yeah, that and much more, Jord," Harley agreed, dreadfully.

"Oh, one last thing, Tess also read somewhere that the only person who could reverse this curse is the one who had seen the Old Hag's face and survived it."

As they entered the library, the first few steps felt heavy, like crossing into another era. The air was thick with dust and time, and Harley hoped it held the answers needed. Her heart raced at the thought of what was about to be uncovered, the truths she hoped could save her life. Shunning any more thoughts, she let the door close behind them.

Jordan looked scared and turned to her, "did you see its face?" She asked curiously.

"Yes."

Jordan wrapped her arm around her friend's shoulder for moral support, trying to be as empathetic as she could. Knowing the fear and pain she must carry, the loss of her parents, a grandmother she never had the chance to know, and now Tess.

After eying the isles of bookshelves, Jordan asked, "Where do we even start, and what are we looking for exactly?"

"The first thing," Harley said to Jordan, "find anything between the 1700-1800s that speak of Old Hag`s. You search that, and I will look up ancient curses, genders, and ages just to be sure. Also, we need to find anything about abandoned cabins in this area."

"This thing is toying with me, Jord. She has the power to kill, but I'm still alive, However, from what I understood after reading, the targeted, has to be on the Hags killing grounds; otherwise, she can only wound them.

As the girls started to separate to find the information, Jordan asked,

"Oh, what about the runes you mentioned?"

"We will look that up together," Harley replied.

While she was scanning the books in the witchcraft section, an older lady with jet-black hair bunched in a messy bun approached her.

"Can I assist with anything?" she asked.

"No, thank you," Harley replied politely.

The lady stood staring at her, not saying a word, making her feel awkward. Harley stared back, analyzing the woman, thinking she was in her mid-forties, and had familiar eyes.

"I'm the Head Librarian here at Bayville. What you seek is interesting," she said, placing a book in its place on the shelf. "We only keep a minimal selection of this research here. Not many come in for ancient information like this." Leaning closer to Harley, she whispered, raising an eyebrow, "The intriguing stuff is locked in the library's attic. If you want, I can show you."

Harley wondered why the Librarian was so helpful about the subject, but kept it to herself.

"Okay, that would be helpful," she said.

"Good, I'll take you there now," the lady whispered eagerly. Come with me."

Harley followed with some hesitation.

"Come along," the woman said, smiling, and patted Harley's shoulder, "Don't be scared; attics can contain answers to many mysteries."

Jordan looked up from the computer as they passed her.

"Hey, where are you going?" she asked.

"*Shhh…*," the Librarian looked and motioned at Jordan with a finger to her lips.

"She's just showing me another section where I may find something," Harley replied.

"Oh, okay," Jordan whispered, "see you in a bit."

"Up this way," the woman said, pointing.

"Is there a brighter light in this stairwell?" Harley asked as she glared up at the dim hallway.

"Sorry, we keep this dim so it doesn't pique the interest of our patrons."

Harley walked ahead after the lady unhooked a black strap guarding the stairs. At the top landing was a light brown wooden door; she approached and tried to open it.

"*The Librarian must keep it locked*," she thought.

"One second," the woman spoke out from behind her.

Harley jumped.

"Heck, you scared me," she said, looking angry. "That was a heck of a whisper."

"Sorry," the librarian replied, pulling a key from the chain around her neck." Let me unlock it. We must keep many things locked here; you never know who may go nosing around."

She continued to give her an unsettling feeling,

"Well, hopefully, I can find what I need quickly."

"Yes, I'm sure you will," the librarian replied, and scanned the area behind her before turning the attic light on. "I can only give you 30 minutes," the lady said. "The attic is my hidden craft area, where I keep things of importance that I have found over the years. These items are not for regular shelves; no one knows what they may reveal. It is an area for selected people like you," she stated, and then left the room, leaving her alone.

The librarian's mysterious persona left her feeling intrigued for a bit while she scanned the dim area.

"*Creepy*," Harley thought, as she moved around.

She couldn't see the other end; it was too dark. Turning, she immediately felt like something was watching her but shook it off, thinking she was just being paranoid and walked deeper into the attic.

Downstairs, Jordan was also deep in her research. Skimming through websites about Witches during the early centuries. She came across many informative articles, but something else instantly caught her attention. It was the same article Harley mentioned Tess finding before her death. Saddened by the thought, she started fidgeting in her seat.

A cool breeze brushed over her. Jordan arched her back and looked around, feeling like something was standing behind her. Seeing nothing, she turned back to the computer, continued reading, and decided to print the article along with a few others.

As she approached the printer, the assistant offered her help; a few students looked up from their tables.

Blushing with a smile, Jordan replied, quietly,

"Thank you anyway; I know how to work the printer."

 Feeling undermined and annoyed, she returned to her seat with the articles and began reading one. The headline intrigued her to read in detail,

***Girl is dead but no body found**, Danvers Massachusetts,*

They believed their daughter was staying at a cabin on the outskirts of the town; her parents thought she might have been ill because they had not heard from her in a while. The local police said that the case needed more investigation.

"Huh, that was short and sweet," she whispered.

Saving the other articles for later, she stood up, folded them, and sat in a nearby armchair with a book she picked up along the way.

"A comedy romance novel," she opened the book to chapter one, and whispered,

 "I may as well read something I enjoy; I could be waiting a while," and then drifted into the story.

VII

Back in the attic, tables of old books and large paintings leaned against the walls to the left side of the room. In the distance, Harley could see something glimmering, but not enough to know what it was. She moved casually and walked further in, ensuring not to bump into anything.

"Who collects this much stuff? I'd need a decade to rummage through all of it," she whispered.

Sucking in her gut, she squeezed through a narrow space between the old wooden bookshelves to reach the far end of the room.

Once there, a slight cloud of dust stirred as she picked up a book from one of the metal tables. Blowing off the remainder of the dust, she read the title:

"A Family Affair." Flipping it over to read the description on the back.

"Hmm, sounds like an interesting read, but not what I'm looking for today," and gently placed the book back.

Curiously, she continued to search deeper into the attic, leading her to one of four antique red pine chests, each adorned with a warm, iridescent glimmer of gold, she muttered,

"What are these?"

As Harley leaned in for a closer look, an ancient inscription caught her eye. It was etched just above the black hanging locks, but it was in a language she didn't speak fluently. Wishing now, that Jordan had come with her.

Spanish again, ugh.

Harley quickly pulled her phone from her back pocket and snapped pictures. All the locks hung open, she kneeled before them, removing the first one and sifted through the chest revealing tons of old documents, and grabbed as many as she could before something made her stop and turn her head.

Glancing around, all that could be seen, were bits of worn-out furniture scattered throughout the area, bookshelves filled with dusty books and magazines, and a table stacked with beige newspapers, that surely featured stories long forgotten.

The dilapidated walls seemed to close in; their surfaces were adorned with peeling wallpaper, that had once been vibrant but now faded into muted patterns. Dark secrets lying dormant within the old attic walls.

"If they could whisper," Harley thought, shivering at her thought.

After a few moments of deep observation, she began rummaging again and then paused. Feeling something hard near the bottom of the chest, she pulled out the item. It was a square, black wooden box featuring a picture of an old log cabin with a white porch and dark, broken windows. The wooded cabin appeared worn, with a dark mossy buildup.

And then, something else caught her attention.

"Eerie," she murmured, her gaze lingering on the green, bony fingers sketched around the top corners of the box.

A sudden realization struck her: looking at the image, made every horrifying incident seem more real. Chills cooled her spine.

"Coincidence or what," Harley thought, nervously.

The title on the box read,

"Den of the Hag: Dare You Enter."

Her eyes widened in shock. She dropped the box and began to back away slowly.

"Déjà vu," she whispered, as fragments of her dreams flooded her mind. "If I was ever a skeptic, I certainly am not anymore. I should have believed Tess." *What in the world was my family involved in?*

Harley's instincts were telling her to leave, but she knew she was on the right path to finding the answers she needed.

As she bent down to grab the box again, she heard something in the corner of the room. Startled, she quickly looked to see what it was, but it was too dim.

"Hello, is someone there?" she asked anxiously, her words hanging in the dusty air.

She moved slowly in the direction, but there was no response, the noise stopped. Hesitating, she quietly and cautiously took a few more steps when another sound caught her attention; this time, it sounded like someone was scratching at the wall.

"Hey, if someone's in here, you need to leave, only one person allowed in the attic at a time. You'll be in trouble; you shouldn't be here," she called out as she thought about the door being locked.

Harley listened again and shouted louder,

"YOU NEED TO LEAVE!"

But hearing only her echo, she thought it might be a rodent. Shaking her head,

This place is pretty run down.

Turning back, Harley quickly collected the box she had dropped, found a table with a book holder, and placed it carefully. She took her time and delicately unlatched the clamps on the side. Upon opening it, a familiar item fell out causing her to tremble while visions of Tess flooded her mind.

"It can't be," she whispered, cupping her mouth in disbelief. "How did this get in here?"

There lay an old tarot card on the table; she picked it up, and this time, she turned her phone light on, pointing it around the room, feeling as though someone was messing with her.

A sick prank.

But she knew it couldn't be,

"It's impossible; I left this exact card in Jordan's closet." she whispered.

Confused, Harley stood there for a few more minutes, trying to make sense of the object before her. After some time, she wiped a bead of sweat from the back of her neck, shoved the card into her pocket and focused on the box sitting in front of her.

Okay, book, what can you tell me?

As frightened as she was to read any of it, Harley was ready for her answers, and gently pulled the book from the box. Looking down at the gold rimmed, light brown pages laying snugly under the historical parchment cover, she whispered,

"It's in considerable condition."

Setting the book in the holder, she flipped it open and glanced at the date.

"1650," she read, and curiously began scanning through the pages.

Spell after spell, overwhelming her. Harley paused for a moment, clenching her burning eyes before continuing. As she continued through the pages, she stopped at a title of interest:

"The Riveting Old Curse."

What's this about? she pondered, shining the light from her phone closer to the text. "It looks like Spanish again; I seriously need to improve my skills."

Frustrated now, Harley sighed at the time on her watch before quickly skimming more of the pages, with nothing popping out.

Not wanting to leave the book behind, she stuffed it down her pants, covering it with her hoodie and started walking toward the entrance.

As she passed the pictures leaning against the wall, one fell, creating a loud bang, causing her to race forward. Stumbling, she landed on her hands and knees, the book wedging painfully into her torso, causing her to cry out in pain.

Frozen for a moment, Harley listened intently and then pushed herself to her feet, dusting off her hands and rubbing her stomach. She examined the room carefully and made her way to the fallen picture. Picked it up gently and leaned it back in place.

Turning to walk away, she stopped suddenly and turned back to the picture, shining her light on it. In that moment, a vision of a woman with deep, dark eyes stared back at her. The portrait looked from the early 1800`s, with the woman sitting on an old brown chair; her face was serious, as if caught in severe pain. She looked frail, relishing a haunting sorrow.

"Maybe 55 or 60." she thought, and somehow portrayed a resemblance to someone, but was unable to know for sure.

White hair in a bun, sat high on the middle of the woman's head, strands hanging near the sides of her pale cheeks; the only color jumping out at Harley were red lips, making her face dramatically paler. A rusty rouge color dress with gold trim covered her whole body, leaving only her hands and black healed boots exposed. Her nails caught Harley's attention; they were a dark green painted, long and pointy, similar to the box she picked up earlier.

Harley stared intensely, into the woman's sad, hollow eyes when the unexpected urge to flee for her life struck her.

As she watched the woman's hand begin to move slowly, she quickly backed away, blinking to clear her vision, not believing what she was seeing.

 As the rest of the portrait continued to manifest, it let out a familiar high-pitched, crackling moan that she never wanted to hear again. The air became cold, while watching the woman's green nails start to protrude from the portrait and reach for her arm.

Screaming frantically, Harley bolted in the opposite direction, racing toward the door. Not looking back, she heard more eerie chuckles, this time so close that the sound pierced deep into her eardrum. Lowering her head and cupping her ears, she screamed until the pain subsided.

After a few seconds, Harley dropped her shaky hands and then swatted at her ear as a cold breath brushed against it. She quickly grabbed and turned the door handle, but it wouldn't budge.

It's jammed, she panicked, pulling harder in desperation.

Now hearing footsteps approaching behind her. One dragging foot after another, creaking floor board after board, closer and louder.

She continued wrestling with the doorknob, pulling with every ounce of strength she had left, until she realized everything went quiet.

Harley gently loosened her trembling grip, trying not to make a sound. She stood motionless, praying the danger was gone. But just as she thought she was safe, a sharp pain shot down the middle of her neck, jolting her stiff. She cried out as her head was yanked back by her ponytail.

"Help me! Get me out!" she screamed, fearing her fate.

Feeling like she was about to pass out, Desperation creeped as she continued pulling at the door, the intensity of her panic increasing by the second.

Exhausted but with one last attempt, she began to kick the door furiously, until suddenly it swung open, sending her crashing into the hallway, where she landed directly on top of the librarian.

"What is wrong with you? Get off me!" the librarian whispered, pushing her as they both scrambled to their feet.

"I thought I was locked in!" Harley replied, breathless.

"Why would you think that?" The librarian asked, frowning.

"We have never had a problem with that door. It must have been how you were turning the handle. Anyway, your time is up; someone else needs the attic."

Harley rubbed the back of her neck as she felt the burning and started to walk away quickly, still trembling,

"Okay, thank you for your help.

 Looking down at her stomach, Harley wrapped her arms around her waist so no one would see the bulge of the book,

"Thank God, she didn't feel it when I landed on her," she mumbled.

Harley swiftly descended the stairs, the heat in her cheeks was a complete giveaway, but she wasn't about to return the book. When she made it to the lower landing, she could see Jordon sitting in a chair reading something,

"What did you get there?" Harley asked.

 Jordan looked up.

"What the heck took you so long?" She responded.

"Another time, Jord, Harley replied, avoiding her question. "Let's get out of here."

Grabbing Jordan's arm, she quickly headed to the exit door.

"Hurry," Harley whispered.

"What the heck is wrong?" Jordan asked.

 "Just hurry, okay? We need to get out of here."

As they started to jump in the car, Harley whipped the book onto Jordan's seat.

Jordan grabbed it, "What's this."

"You can look at it once we get home Jord; just hold onto it tight and don't let anyone see it."

Jordan looked at her friend with anxiousness and sat unsettled for the drive home.

VIII

Jordan stared at the book on the island after throwing it down.

"So, what's it about," she asked, as she grabbed two glasses from the cupboard.

"I'm not sure yet, something about runes and spells, things like that," Harley answered.

"I need to read it, I think it may contain many of my answers. But first, can you tell me what these say? she asked, showing Jordan the pictures she took of the chests in the attic.

"It's a Spanish phrase," Jordan replied, "in English it reads, Shielded by white energy. Whatever that means."

"I'm not sure either," Harley shook her head, frustrated.

"Don't you think we should go to the police about Tess," Jordan asked sadly.

"Not a chance," Harley replied, giving Jordan a serious look, "I mean it, Jord, not a chance; they will think I'm crazy; we can barely believe it; why would the cops? Besides, her body vanished; they may think I did something."

Jordan poured red wine as she continued.

"I have to figure this out on my own, and I get it if you want to run the other way, Jordan. I never wanted to involve any of my friends. Tess was persistent, as I explained."

Jordan passed Harley's glass, and with a big sigh, replied,

"Don't worry, I'm in, let's get reading."

Harley grabbed the book from the counter, and the girls walked to their usual place by the pool. At first, she hesitated, her heart racing as she considered the implications. The curse that haunted her family had grown stronger, creeping into their lives like a relentless shadow. If this book held the key to breaking it, what was she willing to risk to unlock its secrets? But she shunned all the negative thoughts and quickly grabbed it from her friend.

Jordan leaned closer, reading the title,

"The Den of the Hag?"

"I believe it contains relevant information about witchcraft," Harley replied. "It covers topics like curses and reversals, tarot, and runes, tracing back to ancient times, similar to the curse my family is said to have. I think the runes I saw in my dream are a sign that I need them; hopefully, they will help me against this sinister Old Hag. These messages seem to come from beyond. As for the tarot cards, they are revealing more to me, but I'm still trying to understand exactly what that is."

Jordan could see the uncertainty in her friend's face.

Just then, Jan appeared from around the side entrance,

"What are you girls up to today? What mischief is lurking?" she smirked.

Both the girls jolted up, surprised, and answered at high volume, "*NOTHING…*"

Harley quickly slid the book onto her lap, hiding it from Jordan's mom.

"Hum, what's this, Jordan?" her mom asked, ignoring their outburst.

"What?" Jordan asked quickly, her face blushing.

Harley was now feeling a sense of panic, thinking Jordan's mom had seen the book.

Staring at them curiously for a moment, Jan finally pointed at the bottle on the table,

 "I believe you opened one of my old wines; she said, "You must be celebrating something pretty amazing."

They both relaxed in their chairs, with a long sigh, relieved, "No, there's nothing to celebrate here, Miss. Bozzelli." Harley stated, "I mean Jan, just a quiet afternoon by the pool with a great glass of wine made by a fantastic, amazing, independent woman."

"Yeah, nothing interesting in our lives, mom," Jordan endorsed her friend's statement, lowering her eyes to her glass, hoping her mother wouldn't see her red cheeks. She hated lying to her. "You just make the best wine in Massachusetts, that's all."

"Sucking up won't get you ladies a second bottle," she joked, "don't drink too many; you know how bad the headaches are the next day, especially with my homemade stuff," chuckling as she started for the patio door.

"See ya later, Mom", Jordan hollered, as Jan walked into the house.

"I just ran in to grab my wallet, I forgot it this morning. I had my spa treatment and now to the restaurant; maybe sucking up will, however, get you two something from the menu this evening, perhaps a few of my finest entrée`s that serve well with red wine," Jan said winking, as she waved and went inside, Adios, girls."

"That was close," Jordan whispered as she lowered her forehead to the table. "Let's wait and make sure she leaves through the front."

Harley regained her composure and opened the book, after they were sure Jan had left. She flipped through the fragile pages, and felt a tightening in her chest—a reminder of the cost of such power.

Headings leaped out at her, one after another, some in Spanish. She grabbed her phone for google translation while Jordan sat silently listening. And then dropped her phone to continued scanning through more pages until she stopped and whispered the next title.

 "Tarot Cards."

She wanted to explore more to have a deeper understanding of what they all meant, but before reading, she jumped up.

"That reminds me,"… Harley said.

"What?" Jordan asked excitedly, "And you could have just asked me to translate, Harley, you didn`t need Google."

"Sometimes I like to do things for myself, Jord. No offense. Anyway, I have something familiar," she replied, "wait there," hollering as she ran upstairs.

 She entered the room, reaching for the card hidden deep in the closet, and then ran back downstairs, taking her seat next to Jordan.

"Look at this," and threw the card next to the other one on the table. "This is the one the old keeper gave me at the tomb, and pointed to the one laying on the table, that, is the one that fell out of the book. "Do you see the difference, Jordan?"

"No, I don't," she responded, and I thought you got rid of that when mom found it."

Harley looked at her seriously,

"Really Jord? We need them, I stuffed it back in my pocket."

"Swift," Jordan smiled.

"Look at the hands, Harley continued. "They are the exact same cards, only the hands are different. The first card has hands of bones, and the second one, the hands are dark green and wrinkled." I believe they were used while accidentally conjuring The Old Hag.

"So, you truly believe that one of your living ancestors conjured her? They might have been trying to reach out to your deceased ancestor, using tarot cards or other methods, right?" Jordan pressed, seeking clarity.

“Yes, and the hands of bones must represent my deceased grandmother, while the green wrinkled ones belong to the Old Hag. But I need to be sure," she stated. “Also, when I was up in the library attic, I stumbled across a large portrait of an older female resting against the wall; I kept hearing strange sounds, and when I moved ahead to investigate, the figure in the portrait seemed to come to life, reaching her hands out to grab me, they resemble these hands in the card,” Harley tapped it, “and then I ran, she said."

Jordan's eyes widened, as she sat silently listening to the events of the attic.

 "I must say, that is some story. Harley. Either you're just fooling with me or losing your mind again," Jordan giggled. “However, your stories do scare me a wee bit, you have a very vivid imagination. You should write a book,” she joked.

"Believe it or not, Jord, it happened, and this is exactly why Tess is not with us," she snapped.

"Geez," Jordan said, “some of your story just seems a little out there,” and took a sip of wine.

"It's true,” Harley replied softly, “sorry for snapping."

"Well, what's next?" Jordan asked curiously, still not convinced of everything Harley said she witnessed in the library attic.

“Nothing's really clear yet,” she replied; “I need more answers. One thing I do know for sure, is that everything is happening from beyond the grave, Jordan, and when you can`t see something, how do you end it?"

Jordan asked, "We know your grandmother was involved but what about the woman in the library attic portrait, who is she, and could she have been involved?"

"Honestly Jord, I`m not sure if there is a connection, I believe I was being tormented," she replied, shaking her head. "My family is haunted by an old curse. We have the tarot cards, mentioning`s the runes, and now this mysterious old book. And let's not overlook the vivid dreams I've been having. It`s all pointing to one sinister thing, that Witch, and I`m sure Tess died by its hands, somehow."

Harley locked eyes with Jordan, desperation etched on her face.

 "We have to put a stop to this, Jord. If we don't, I could be the next victim."

Jordan put her glass down and ran to hug her. "Your mom never hinted at anything before she passed away?" she asked caringly.

"Nope, not a thing. I'm not sure how much she even knew," Harley replied.

Harley's eyes fixed on the pages again; she wiped a tear as she continued investigating while Jordan searched on her phone. Another title popped out, causing her to bite hard on her lip. With a quick flash of Tess's dead body, she read the title loudly.

"YOUR NOSE WILL BE YOUR DEATH,"

and then slammed the book closed, making Jordan gasp.

"HELL! Why do you always do that," Jordan yelled, dropping her phone and grabbing her chest. "Damn, your lip is bleeding, Harley." Jumping up, Jordan ran to grab a tissue from the counter. "Here, dab it," she ordered, and slid back into her seat.

"Sorry, just a horrible memory of Tess and her nosing around," Harley replied, as she dabbed her wound, hesitating to open the book again.

Jordan grabbed it.

"My turn," she said, eagerly, as she flipped through the pages, and sat up tall. "Look, Harley, "it says right here," pointing as she read the words, "Reversals.

"To reverse an ancient curse, you need to enter the Old Hags Den with the 13 Runes and say this reversal spell: It also says, this is dangerous. Do not attempt this alone, and always have an escape plan."

Jordan jumped up, backing away from the book.

"No way am I entering some psycho Hags home, she could put a spell on me."

"Here, look," Harley cut in, pointing out another spell for protection before entering. "However, it states that it may or may not work and to enter at your own risk."

Harley gulped hard, scared to read ahead; she closed the book.

"We need a break and a good plan," she said, looking at Jordan's frightened face.

As both girls were deep in thought, the front door flew open, startling them again.

"Hey, hey, my Señioritis," Enzo approached the table, "what's this?" picking up the book.

Jordan quickly pulled it from his hands,

"Nothing of your concern," she replied.

Harley spoke up,

"Actually, it just might be Jord." Looking Enzo up and down. "You're a pretty strong guy, right, Enz?" She asked, now smirking.

Totally out of character, she reached up and grabbed his bicep, more relaxed now, thinking the wine might be hitting her harder than she had realized.

"Sure, maybe," Enzo replied, blushing, and started checking out his biceps. "Why, do you like what you see?" lifting his eyebrows.

"Okay, you two, stop fooling around." Jordan interrupted.

"I'm serious, Jord." Harley gave her a wink; we could use him".

"Huh," Jordan replied, confused. "He wouldn't believe any of this, besides using him for what, BAIT," she chuckled.

"Wait, I'm lost," Enzo said, looking from girl to girl, "what are you both joking about?"

"We need your help," Harley answered.

"Are you sure about this, Jordan asked her?"

 "More than sure," she replied.

Enzo ran his fingers through his hair. "Vale que pasa?" he asked.

Harley looked at Jordon for the meaning.

"Okay, what's up," Jordan said, rolling her eyes, "Speak English, Enz; she can't keep up."

"Ha, funny, Jord," Harley remarked sarcastically. "This is serious, Enzo, and I will explain everything to you; take a seat."

As Enzo did what he was told, Harley looked at Jordan.

"We need to have a plan," she stated, "and I now have one," nodding in Enzo's direction. "You may not like it, Jord, but let's keep Tess in mind as you hear what I'm thinking."

"What about Tess?" Enzo cut in curiously. "Come to think of it, I haven't heard from her for some time. Have either of you?"

Harley stared awkwardly at Enzo for a moment.

"I will start with Tess, Enzo," and she told him everything about the graveyard, the old keeper, the attic, all of it.

 Enzo kept getting up from his seat to pace, running his fingers through his bangs.

"No way. Tess dead? I don't believe it; where's her body?" demanding an answer. "Have you called the cops?"

 "I already asked that, Enzo," Jordan replied, annoyed.

He stared at her, confused.

Looking at his reaction, Harley knew he would be hard to convince, but having Jordan back her story would make it easier; she looked at her friend for help.

"I know how you're feeling, Enzo. I couldn't accept it either, when Harley told me," Jordon cut in, but it's true, at least I think," she said, hesitating. "I thought Harley was losing her mind at first, but I know she wouldn't make up a sick story like this. Would you, Harley?" Shooting her friend a disturbed look.

Harley thought as she listened to her friends;

the sure thing about Jordan was her glowing innocence, which attracted anyone's trust.

"I don't even know what to say to this," Enzo said, getting her attention. "Wow, Tess, it can't be true," he repeated mournfully. "And this suggestion of an Old Hag, seems a bit crazy."

Harley replied,

"I was just with Tess a few days ago, Enzo. I know what I saw. It was just before I passed out in the graveyard, and it's not something I desire to remember, but I do."

"So, what help do you need from me," he asked hesitantly.

"Yeah, what do we need Enzo for?" Jordan agreed.

"Well, I read somewhere that witches have a profound attraction to men."

Enzo immediately stopped pacing, looked at Harley and dropped his jaw.

"WHAT!" now raising his voice, "*NO WAY*," he said, waving his hand, "I don't want any Old Hag-like thing horny for me; what if it puts a curse on me or worse."

"That's what I said," Jordan replied, "but we can't let her do this alone; it's too dangerous; it's much better if we stay together like a pack; there's no other way, Enzo. Besides, Harley has a great plan, with the help of that book she found, right there," Jordan said, patting it. "Let's at least hear her out."

Enzo sat uncomfortably back at the table with the girls,

"We're not a pack of wolves, Jordan" he muttered, annoyed by her comparison. "I don't like this, I don't know what I'm getting myself into, but I will do it for Tess," Enzo agreed.

For a brief moment, both girls witnessed Enzo's teary eyes for the first time. He gave them a quick wipe, as Harley was about to lay out the plan.

IX

"Jord, your mom is always sneaking up on us. Let's go somewhere out of sight, just to be safe," Harley said before she began.

Jordan stood up.

"I have the perfect place," she replied, "let's go," leading the way as Enzo and Harley followed close behind.

Entering the wine cellar, they found it dimly lit. The flickering candlelight cast dazzling sparkles along the old brick walls. Ahead of them, sat a small round table with stools just outside the wine cooler door, and they all took their seat.

"This is perfect," Harley stated, "at least if your mom creeps down here, we can say we were shopping amongst her incredible collection, that would go well with the food she said she was bringing."

"Smart thinking," Enzo agreed, "I'm staying for supper," winking at Jordan.

She rolled her eyes, turning to Harley,

"Okay, what's the plan?"

Harley's heart started pounding heavily in her chest, before she began. She looked around the room, reminding herself of the library incident. The fear of dying from her family's curse was a continuous distraction. She eluded every negative thought at that moment and focused on her idea.

She stared at Enzo momentarily, thinking about how he would handle his request. Shaking it off, Harley didn't care whether he would accept; she was determined to break the curse that had haunted her family for generations. And, although saving her own life was the top of priorities, finding Tess's body and keeping her other friends safe, gave her a heightened surge of motivation.

Jordan set the candle in the center of the table, As the scent of melting Burberry wax filled the air, the atmosphere buzzed with urgency and anticipation.

"Funny question Jord. Why didn't you just use the light," Enzo asked?

"So my mother wouldn't see the lights on Enzo," think with that great brain of yours." Jordon rolled her eyes.

"So, guys," Harley interrupted, "the first thing on the list is to find the old cabin. I`m sure it has a broken-down white porch, as I mentioned to Jordan already."

 "That could be a million homes around here," Enzo intervened, rubbing the back of his neck.

"True," Jordan agreed, "That will be hard to find."

"Well, to the best of my knowledge, it has run-down wooden logs, it's rustic looking, and hopefully, with a white rocking chair on the porch, which will narrow things down a bit; all of the cabins in this location are not identical," she replied. "We need to map out wooded areas."

"True," Jordan agreed; "I'll recheck the articles I printed at the library, make some phone calls, and pretend I'm a journalist revisiting unsolved events."

"The woods?" Enzo questioned, cutting in, perplexed. "How do you know it's in the woods anyway? It could be an old house on the street?"

"Let's just say my dreams do come true on rare occasions, and hopefully, according to my last dream, I'm right in this case," Harley replied, "besides Jordan's article of the missing girl in the woods, fits."

Looking at Jordan, she said, "It will help if you go back to the library and check again for anything you may have missed, not just the articles you have, check deep in the archives. Usually, there will be pictures; I will draw the vision from my dream for you to reference. Hopefully, the librarian doesn't recognize you; she may have already discovered the missing book."

"Great, now I'm worried," Jordan replied, "I'll wear a hat."

"Enzo, I need you to find a good small metal shovel that won't break if it hits something hard."

Jordan and Enzo looked at Harley.

"A shovel? Why do we need it?" they asked, simultaneously.

"Um…," Harley closed her eyes for a moment, allowing the intensity of their task to spread over her. She could already feel their fears intertwining with her own. The thought of the curse was growing stronger; another one of her friends being targeted was causing her more anxiety and making her stomach churn.

She sat up, fidgeting in her seat for a moment, and then revealed the next part of her plan. knowing it would cause chaos among the three of them. Looking back at Enzo, Harley said,

"I need you to dig up my grandmother's grave."

His jaw dropped again.

"Excuse me," he said, wide-eyed. "I didn't hear you right. Did you just say, dig up your grandmother?"

"Yes," she answered boldly.

"Now, I am certain, I agree with Jordan's earlier accusations, that you've completely lost it," he replied, throwing his hands in the air. The irritation in his voice was palpable. "Loca, Loca, Loca," he repeated while staring at Jordan; Harley also looked at her.

"Crazy, crazy, crazy," Jordan repeated. "He thinks you're crazy, Harley, and I agree," she said, stunned at her friend's unreasonable demand.

"We have to. I need something from the grave, as I mentioned before, Jord. This is what Tess and I started; I need to finish it."

"What could you possibly need from a dead person?" Jordan asked.

Again, Harley hesitated; and decided to keep that part to herself until the right moment.

"I just need something significant to reverse this curse. Don't you realize I'm also afraid for both of you? Look what happened to Tess. I would never put you in this position if it wasn't extremely important, I know how horrible it all sounds."

She put her hands to her face and started crying.

Compassion overwhelmed Enzo as he leaped into the seat next to Harley and wrapped his arms around her, cradling her tightly,

"*Shhh*, it's okay; you don't need to cry," he said, softly. "We're going to help, right?" staring at Jordan.

Jordan gulped her wine down hard and patted her friend's hand.

"Yeah," she agreed, "as much as I don't want to see human remains, of course, we will help, for you and Tess."

Harley knew Jordan would eventually regret those words. But, at that moment, the three friends nodded in unison, their resolve solidifying like the wax pooling at the base of the candle. As daunting as it was, they had each other's back.

After a few minutes, Harley wiped her eyes.

"Sorry for breaking down, I just want this to end. I wish Tess would never have found any information, but it doesn't matter what I wish now; I need to take care of it, once and for all."

Jordan piped up,

"So, now that we are given our assignments, what are you doing?" And, by the way, Enzo has an easy job," she whined. "Finding a shovel, really Harley? But then she immediately took back her complaint, "well, it's easy for now, I guess."

Jordan looked at Enzo with sorrow, picturing him digging up a grave, being the first to see what lay inside, she almost heaved at the thought; cupping her mouth, and lowered her head.

"Enzo, after you get the proper shovel, I need you to text me, and I will tell you exactly where to meet us; we won't need it right away; just leave it in your trunk."

"Won't fit," he blurted, "my car is too small."

"The shovel will be small, Enzo", Jordan replied, annoyed.

"Have you seen my trunk Jordan," he laughed.

"Okay, so just walk, you're not far," Harley said, "leave it at the side of the house, somewhere Jordan's mom won't find it, in the bushes; I'll grab it."

"Sure, I got it. I'll text you in a bit. I'm sure our gardener has something in the shed out back; if not, I'll buy one."

"NO!" Harley yelled, as he started to leave the table.

"What, why not?" he asked, turning to her.

"Because that's a paper trail, she answered, "If anything goes wrong, I don't want the police's involvement; if we have to leave the shovel behind, it could potentially help their investigation and lead them to us."

"Oh, right, makes sense," he replied, and started up the cellar stairs. "No purchase, leave it with me, don't worry; I'll find one."

As the girls continued talking, Enzo peeked around the cellar wall,

"Hey Jord, your mom doesn't have a shovel, eh?" he asked, with a grin.

Jordan rolled her eyes, "Does my backyard look like it needs a shovel? It's all made of cement; look around on your way out, Enzo," she answered, sarcastic.

 "Okay, okay, just joking," he said, smirking, "text you soon," and then disappeared for the second time.

Jordan watched Harley pull out her phone and press the maps app.

"Hey, weird question; what happened to the shovel you and Tess were using?"

She looked at her, "I left it, Jordan. While being chased by an Old Hag, that moment didn't seem fit to worry about a garden spade." she replied rudely.

Jordan didn`t look amused.

"I guess so," she said, "I didn`t think about that."

"Sorry, Jord, I`m always snapping at you, while you're only trying to help, I'm just stressed. Tess had a garden spade in the car. I used to dig a good-sized hole and use my hands at times."

"Oh, that must have been horrible." Jordan, shook her head in dismay.

Harley could see her friends fear, but it wasn't the right time to console her. She had to stay strong.

"It was torturous, Jord, but I'm doing it right this time. That's why I sent Enzo for another shovel: to get the morbid job done quickly and choose one he likes since he's doing the digging."

Harley stood up from her seat,

"Jordan, no matter what happens to me when we get to this place, I want you to run. Promise me you will run, and please make Enzo leave with you."

"No way, I won't do that," Jordan replied angrily, "besides, Enzo will never listen to me, so don't even ask that."

Harley made her expectations clear: "I'm not asking Jordan; I'm telling. This was my family, my curse, my problem. You have your mom Jord; and she wouldn`t be able to bear your loss, if anything happened to you, I'm not trying to scare you. I'm just thinking of Tess."

Jordan stared at Harley and listened carefully to her reasoning.

"I couldn't live with myself if I survived, and god forbid something happened to either of you, Jord; besides, my parents are gone; I have nothing to leave behind, but you do," she said sternly.

Jordan stayed silent as Harley searched Google on her phone and took that as a queue to get started with her assignment.

"One last question" Jordan asked as they stood up to leave. "What's the rest of the plan?"

"All in time, Jord," she answered. "It will all fall into place once we have everything we need and know exactly where we are going to end up."

Once upstairs, Jordan grabbed her car keys and purse,

"I'll be back later; I have some work to do, Boss," she joked as they walked through the house. "Hopefully I find something more," and then walked out, leaving Harley alone.

Taking a seat at the armchair in the living room, Harley continued searching for news of missing persons in the area.

"Huh, what's this?" she whispered; the headline read,

Local Forest discovered two female bodies,

FBI were called in, but they had no leads, and the scene was too gruesome to reveal any further details to the public.

She dropped her phone in her lap, remembering how bad Tess looked before she passed out.

"Could they be connected?" she wondered, "why am I still alive?" She picked up her phone and looked at the date, *1998*.

"Old news," Harley thought, as she searched for more articles. Scrolling through, another headline caught her interest:

Local Forest death*, one female body found so gruesome, they wouldn't mention, the year 2000, and again, no leads.*

"This has to be the place; this was only a year ago," Her gut flipped, she knew this was it, "I have to get there," she whispered, feeling the hair on her arms rise, as she stood.

Entering Jordan's room, she sat at the desk, switched on the computer, and typed in the headlines she found on her phone. Looking through the article one last time to find the exact location, it wasn't mentioned; she brought up Google again, this time typing in *Old Hags, death, local forest*, and finally, the words jumped out:

'THE FOREST OF RUNES.'

She quickly slammed the laptop and felt a wave of fear flow through her whole body, taking a deep breath, Harley reached with a shaky hand to open the computer again, hoping it didn't break, she looked at the name, and searched for the location of the forest. Speaking into her phone this time,

"Where is the forest of Runes?"

Google results returned quickly:

It`s located in a small town called Alem, Massachusetts.

She looked at the maps app and discovered something unsettling,

"Only 10 kilometers from the graveyard," she whispered.

The bedroom door suddenly flew open, scaring her.

"Hi, Harley," Jordan's mom peered her head into the room, making Harley shut the laptop quickly. "Is Jordan in here?" she asked, looking around.

"No, Miss Bozzelli, she had to run an errand. I'm just using her laptop, my phone is slow, and then I'm off as well," she replied.

"Oh, that's too bad; I brought home some amazing food from the restaurant for you girls to try, it`s a new recipe I conjured up."

The words set Harley aback.

Conjured,

Thinking of the curse, she quickly brushed away the horrifying thought.

"That's so nice of you, she admitted. "I will text Jord and let her know; maybe we can have some later when we get home. I'm meeting her back here."

"Sure, that would be nice," she replied. "If I'm not up, it will be in the warmer, and, I told you before, call me Jan; I`m too young to be called Miss," she chuckled and shut the door.

"Thanks for the food, Jan," Harley hollered.

She hid the book under her hoodie again so Jordan's mom wouldn't see it on her way out, grabbed her keys from the counter, ran to her car, quickly texted Enzo, and Jordan, telling them where to meet her—Somewhere she was dreading, a place she thought she would only have to visit in a dream.

X

Harley pulled into the graveyard's parking lot and looked around. She found Enzo leaning on his car checking his cell phone. Pulling up beside him, she rolled her window down,

"I need you guys to follow me when Jordan pulls in; change of plans," she said.

Enzo nodded, "What's taking her so long? Did she text you?

"Ya, I think she took the wrong street; she shouldn`t be much longer," Harley replied.

"She always takes a wrong turn," Enzo mumbled, sounding impatient.

As Harley started to defend Jordan, she pulled in, and Enzo anxiously motioned her to follow them as he jumped back in his vehicle. All three cars pulled out. Harley quickly typed in the Forest of Runes on her GPS and checked her rear-view mirror to see both cars were close behind. GPS showed a detour was needed,

"Damn," she uttered, as a tense expression spread over her face, "this will take longer, and the sun is already starting to set."

A while later, Harley pulled into a gravel parking area at the right of the forest entrance where all three parked. Jumping out first, she asked,

"Hey Enzo, do you have a flashlight in your car?"

"Nope, sorry, don't carry one."

"I have a lantern. Will that work?" Jordan asked.

"Something's better than nothing," Harley replied, "The sun is going down; it will be dark soon."

"Well, let's move quickly," Enzo said, "I don't much like dark forests.

 Hearing the mumble of his words, both girls looked in his direction, watching him run his fingers through his bangs."

 "What? they asked, sarcastically, a strong guy like you, scared?"

"Nooo, not at all," he tentatively replied, "just don't like them."

"Remember what we talked about Enzo," Jordan urged, her eyes fierce as she glared at him. "We're in this together. No matter what happens, we'll face it as one," slamming her trunk closed.

Jordan looked at Harley and smirked, unsure and thinking that Enzo would never protect them when it began to get tough.

 "Let's get going," Harley said, as Jordan lit the lantern.

 "Why do you have a lantern in your car anyway, Jord?" Enzo asked.

"I bought it the other day for the backyard. I imagined it hanging in the far seating area would look nice."

 The three came to a halt at the opening.

 "Who's going first?" Jordan asked, nervously, staring into the shaded surroundings.

 "I'll go," Harley said and grabbed the lantern from her.

"Okay, I'll go in last to watch behind," Enzo said, reluctantly.

Jordan rolled her eyes,

"Okay, ya, Enzo, you do that."

As they wandered into the forest, the sun was setting faster than Harley had hoped.

"Look," Jordan said and stopped abruptly, making Enzo bump into her. She flew forward and landed on the ground.

"OW," she cried.

"Woah, sorry, Jordan, didn't mean to do that," Enzo said, leaning down next to her.

"Be more alert," she snapped as he helped her stand.

"Are you okay, Jordan?" Harley asked, pointing to the blood on her hand.

"Yeah, I'm fine," she said, wiping it on Enzo's shirt.

"Hey, what was that for?" he asked, annoyed.

"To remind you to be more careful next time," she shot back.

"Hey, you two, keep it down," Harley whispered. "Hush, do you hear that?"

All became quiet except for the wind's low howls through the mingling tree branches.

"No, what do you hear?" Jordan whispered back.

"I could have sworn I heard some light music in the distance," she answered.

"Maybe just echoes from the wind; it seems to be picking up a bit," Enzo affirmed or an animal, but don't worry," he said, "I have my pocket knife."

The girls turned to look at him, shaking their heads.

"Anyways," Jordan spoke up, "As I was trying to say before someone rudely knocked me to the ground, look at the sign wedged into the shrubs there."

Harley walked closer, shining the light over the sign.

"Yup, this is the right place," she said, moving her body aside so Jordan and Enzo could read it as one.

"The Forest of Runes."

Harley continued to walk the trail as they followed.

Enzo stopped abruptly, "listen," he whispered.

"What," the girls asked.

"The night suddenly became extremely quiet," he stated, looking around anxiously.

She and Jordan ignored him and looked back towards the darkened path, then at each other, unsure if they wanted to proceed. And just as Enzo was about to say something. A powerful gust of wind swirled around them and the sky began to crackle with electricity. They stood silently in the center of the darkened forest, the moonlight casting just enough illumination to frighten them by their own shadows.

Looking up, Harley yelled, over the growls of the wind

"Let's go, NOW."

As they moved briskly, deeper into the forest, the moon quickly vanished and raindrops fell.

"We should have grabbed umbrellas," Jordan whined, looking up.

"I didn't think to check the weather, Jord. Given the circumstances, I was thinking about digging up a grave and all," Enzo said sarcastically.

Harley continued searching while Enzo and Jordan continued bickering. As she ran for them, each lightning bolt would reveal another rune.

"Look, you two. I found another, and if you pay attention and help me, we can get this done quickly. Or would you rather be here all night?"Harley said, breathlessly, realizing she sounded more like Tess now.

Enzo and Jordan took her seriously, and simultaneously, alone, each ran to collect a peaking rune, risking their safety while the darkness devoured their every step.

"That cursed lantern," Jordan complained, running back "it's not bright enough; I can't see where I'm stepping." She passed it to Harley.

Harley turned immediately and centered the light on them, "its yes or no, guys, I'm giving you a chance to leave, but I'm going deeper into the forest."

 Enzo and Jordan gulped hard and looked at each other anxiously, saying,

 "Yes, we're in," while shaking their heads no.

Harley turned to lead again, without saying anything more, and they both followed closely behind.

Soon after, Enzo let out a loud squeal.

"What the hell?"

He jumped and turned quickly to look but couldn't see anything but a pop can lying near his foot. Frustrated, he kicked it. Harley ran to him with the light.

"What happened?" she asked.

"I felt something blow on my ear. I swear, I felt it," Enzo replied, as he was swatting at his ear again.

"*Shhh*... calm down, Enz. It's okay. I believe you," Harley reassured him. "The same thing happened to me in the attic of the library, stay very alert!"

"Okay, now I'm extremely creeped out," Jordan whispered, wrapping her arm tightly around Enzo's elbow. "Do you feel that," she asked, sticking her other hand in front of Enzo`s face.

He jerked his head back quickly , "must you?" he asked, annoyed that her finger almost went up his nose.

"The rain stopped," Jordan said, ignoring him, but the lightning is still zipping around us, it's eerie," and then she nudged her elbow into him hard. "Are you sure you're, okay?" She whispered.

"Ow…,I'm fine, Jord, geez," Enzo replied, and said, after composing himself. "You can let go of me now. Maybe just a bug flew near my ear."

Not realizing Jordan grabbed him from her own fear, she knew Enzo was trying to sound tough, but she could feel his body trembling as hard as her own.

"What's worse, is you trying to pick my nose, loca" he joked.

"Gross," she gave him a shove.

Approaching a fork in the path, Harley stopped,

"I don't know the way from here," she said, worried they would get lost.

Enzo pointed towards a sign that lit up with another jolt in the sky,

"There," he said.

Harley ran and wedged herself between the trees, held the lantern up but couldn't read it; it was too high.

"Here, I'll lift you," Enzo leaped toward her.

 She handed the lantern to Jordan. Enzo kneeled and held his hands together,

"Step in, he said."

She hesitated momentarily and asked,

"Are you sure you can hold me, Enz?"

He punched his upper arm, joking, "Didn't you say I had big biceps?"

Harley grinned and then placed her foot into his palms; she pushed herself up using her other foot and steadied herself with the top of his head; she could feel Enzo shaking but ignored it as she reached higher, hoping it was a rune.

"Almost have it," Harley yelled, stretching.

She gave one last hard push on Enzo`s head. Losing her balance, she fell, landing on her back.

 Jordan rushed to her side, screaming, "Are you okay?"

But Harley just lay there with her hands on her chest, rocking back and forth. Her eyes wide as she gasped for air. Enzo watched in dismay and then turned to Jordan,

"How do I help her?"

Ignoring him, Jordan stood helpless, as she watched her friend take another gasp of air, only this time louder, and then finally, the rhythm of her breathing started to steady.

Enzo fell to his knees beside her and lowered his head.

"I'm so sorry, Harley" and started to help her sit up. "I should have caught you."

Harley coughed a few times before speaking,

"It's fine, Enzo," her voice raspy.

He and Jordan helped Harley to her feet, wiping the loose dirt from the back of her sweater.

"Anything else I can do for you?" Jordan asked, anxiously.

"No, Jord. I'm good" she said, coughing again, and then held out the object she grabbed before her fall. "But look what I managed to grab. It's the 6th rune."

"Are they all exactly like the runes found in the book you stole?" Jordan asked.

Harley gave her a stern look,

"Must you tell everyone?" she snapped.

"Sorry," Jordan replied quickly, feeling the heat in her cheeks.

 "So. what do we do with them?" Enzo asked.

"Well, for starters, we need to collect all 13 of them, and I believe we go left at the fork because that's the side of the path we found it. Just keep following them," Harley ordered.

Jordan cried, "It's so dark. I'm unsure if we will find them all, Harley, and I don't want to stay in this horrible place all night."

 "No turning back now, Jordan, we stay on this path," she said, "I need those runes, I will have to stand in the center of the 13; that's the point of them. Once we find them all and scope out the cabin quickly, we can leave."

"I can help her, if you want to return to the car, Jord?" Enzo said.

Jordan looked behind at the narrow, dark trail back to her car and then back at Enzo, wide-eyed,

"I'm the one who said we stay together no matter what, so I stay. Thank you," she answered bluntly and pushed him aside, to walk next to her friend.

"Getting back to Enzo`s question about the runes," Harley replied, "I have to stand in the center of the runes while I say a reversal spell, Enz."

"Look, the runes have pictures," Jordan said, pointing at the one she held.

"Yes, they have symbols and meanings," Harley replied. "I don't know much about them, but that one resembles the moon rune. I remember seeing a picture of it while I was reading about it; it has something to do with power and hidden energy. I also recall it from my dream, so everything is starting to fall into place. Let's find the rest."

As 3 a.m. approached, the weather changed and became quiet again, but the temperature dropped immensely.

"I'm freezing," Jordan cried. "Look, I can see my breath," speaking dramatically and exhaling into the cold air.

"Come closer," Enzo said, as he wrapped his arm around her.

Jordan shoved it off, "forget about it, Enzo, I'll deal with it."

"What…?" he asked, innocently, "I was just trying to warm you up."

"Um, ya right," she replied, rolling her eyes again.

Harley walked ahead of them.

"Wait up, be careful," Enzo yelled.

"Now you care, Enzo, after letting her fall to her near death," Jordan said, exaggerating.

"Hey, I tried Jord," Enzo said, defending himself. "Come here, I'll help you too, I'll keep you nice and warm, his smile widened.

"You guys are too slow, and with all that foreplay," Harley yelled back, jokingly, I have to pick up the slack, grabbing all these runes."

Jordan's eyes bulged. "That's not happening," she stated defensively. "Enzo's just being a pig again, plus I`m trying to help, but I can't see because you're the one with the lantern."

Enzo shot Jordan a smirk,

"Moi," he said, "A pig? Never."

"I'm joking, Jordan. Relax." Harley chuckled. "I didn't know you knew French Enzo," she said, changing the subject because she knew Jordan was embarrassed at her naivety.

"I'm a man of many languages," he replied, as Harley ran to a nearby branch.

 "Hey, why are you running away?" he hollered.

"I thought I saw the last of the runes hanging on a branch over here, but it's not; we have twelve; I need the 13th one."

 "What's the importance of thirteen anyway?" Enzo questioned.

"Besides needing all the runes for the spell, particularly the Algiz rune for protection, the thirteenth rune symbolizes transformation. I hope to draw the Old Hag out from her home of smog, so we can truly understand what we're up against. Additionally, I'm searching for an Ouija board; the planchette will assist me in seeing that evil thing, if she doesn't reveal herself, as she has done so violently in the past."

Enzo immediately regretted asking.

"Oh, that's great. We get to see your ancestor, amazing," he said wryly. "Just what I wanted all my life, to see a crazy cursive Old woman, Hag." He spat and ran his fingers through his hair as he followed the girls closely.

"It's not my ancestor; it was conjured by an ancestor who dabbled in witchcraft, or was possibly a lineage of good witches.

"Maybe we can skip seeing the unseen," Jordan said, agreeing with Enzo.

Harley kept walking ahead, ignoring their complaints. Suddenly, she could feel the unmistakable energy of evil. She stopped for a minute and noticed a shrub like the one in her dream. She hid behind, peeking over it. An old cabin sat in the distance with one lit window. Quickly, she gestured to her friends to hurry.

"*Shhh*..." Harley whispered, "there it is."

Enzo and Jordan joined her behind a dying shrub.

"What if there is someone in there?" Jordan whispered.

"That's probably the case, Jord…, you go first" Enzo said, devilishly.

Jordan elbowed him, "Shut up."

"Would you two be serious?" Harley intervened, "We need to get closer."

Enzo stood to a slouch, "I'll go," he said,, bravely.

Jordan grabbed his arm,

"No way," and pulled him back down. "We stay together."

"Why…? It's the least I can do after letting you fall," he stated. "Besides, Jordan doesn't want to go, and it's just to get close enough to view the grounds, maybe a peak inside."

"Yeah, just let him check it out," Jordan agreed, relieved he was willing to go alone. "You and I can keep watch from here."

Harley thought about it for a few moments, scared to lose another friend, but knew it was time to put past thoughts of Tess to rest, at least for the time being.

"Fine," she answered, "Only if you're sure, Enzo."

Without any response, he took off quickly around the shrub, and in a hunched position, carefully and quietly crept forward toward the old, warped deck.

"Stay safe, Enzo", Jordan whispered, peeking over her shoulder.

"Jordan, I'm not being rude, but if you lean any harder, I'm going to be a permanent part of this shrub," Harley said.

"Sorry," Jordan replied, moving back, "I'm just nervous for him."

Harley's anxiety spiked too, as she watched Enzo creep closer to the house, and soon after, a feeling of warmth ran down her finger,

"Ouch," she cried, as she pulled her finger from her mouth.

"Bad habit, Harley," Jordan mentioned, anxiously.

Harley ignored her and wiped her bloody nail on her sweater.

"Okay, let's get a bit closer, Jordan."

"Huh," she answered, confused, "I think we are close enough. Besides, Enzo wanted to go."

"I can't just kneel here anymore; let's go." She jumped up, startling Jordan, and pulled on her hoodie, "come on, he needs us closer in case something happens," she demanded.

"What the heck can we do to help if something happens?" Jordan asked, while trying to pull away.

"Now is not the time to think too hard, Jord; we'll figure out, if and when later. Right now, Enzo disappeared somewhere, and I can`t see him, so let's go check."

Surrendering, Jordan followed her as they edged closer to the old log cabin.

"Enzo must be around the back," Harley whispered, as they hid behind a large tree, waiting.

At the back of the cabin, Enzo could see two upper windows and a black door at the rear of the cabin.

Are there any lights in this place? he wondered.

As he turned, a towering tree loomed in the distance—the only feature in the dreary yard, covered by, what looked to be soot.

"That's weird," he whispered.

Being nosey, he walked toward the tree, and began to loop around the massive stump, larger than anything he had ever seen. Casting his cell light closer, revealed a mucky dark green moss coat with patches of red, resembling dried blood.

"Sick," he mumbled, squinting his nose and shook his head.

The tree seemed ancient, as if it had witnessed centuries of torture. The long, empty branches swayed in a rhythmic motion, making him ponder:

"Where are the leaves?"

Scanning the ground again, he noticed some kind of animal laying to the right side of the trunk. Creeping in for a closer look, he realized it was a dead rat and then backed away swiftly.

Suddenly, the back door swung open, slamming against the house, and a fierce wind surged toward him, knocking him to the ground. Enzo lay there, paralyzed, feeling a heavy weight on his chest as he struggled to move. Panic surged within him as he opened his mouth to yell, but restricted to only his gasp, he was plagued with terror, he remained frozen in place, the darkness closing in around him.

Harley yelled over the wind when they reached the front of the cabin,

"Wait," and she stopped abruptly; this time, Jordan bumping into her.

"What?" Jordan asked, worried.

"I heard a bang," she said. "Quick, this way."

They ran to the side of the cabin but were stopped in their tracks. Frozen and helpless. They could see Enzo squirming on the ground just a few feet away, shrouded in a dark, thick mist that covered his defenseless body.

Harley began screaming at the unseen force.

"*LEAVE HIM ALONE*! It's me you want, Witch! Come get me!"

Tears welled in her eyes. She wasn't going to lose another friend; this time, she was prepared to face any evil force.

Jordan watched, trembling violently as her friend screamed and tried pushing forward to defend Enzo. Moments felt like hours as the horrifying events unfolded, but something changed as Harley continued to confront the unseen entity—the hold on her started to weaken. Perhaps it was Harley's determination not to give up, or perhaps... *she did inherit the good Witch legacy.*

Suddenly, Jordan found she could move, and Enzo jumped to his feet. Jordan also noticed something she hadn't seen during the dreadful event: an object hanging from a branch of the ancient tree. Her bravery ramped up and she tried to run for it, tripping along the way. Then, something grabbed her from behind, and she screamed...

"*Shhh…*, It's okay, it's me."

Looking up, relieved to see Enzo. He helped her to her feet.

"I see it!" Jordan yelled, as she steadied herself.

 Just then, Harley was lifted and thrown back. Enzo quickly ran to her as Jordan rushed for the rune. He leaned over Harley, who was moaning in pain.

"Get me up," she said urgently. "Hurry!"

Jordan ran back quickly, with the rune. She and Enzo grabbed an arm and swiftly lifted their friend. As Harley tried to balance herself, another loud bang came from the cabin. They all turned to look— this time, the door slammed shut.

"Run!" screamed Jordan.

Enzo stopped at the spot where Harley and Jordan had been attacked and grabbed the lantern.

"*GO*!" he yelled as he turned to keep watch behind them.

"Come on, Enz!" Jordan hollered back. "What are you waiting for?"

He gave one last look before darting toward them, staying close behind the girls until they reached the mouth of the forest where are they all stood breathlessly.

"You didn't get the piece you needed from the Ouija board," Jordan said.

"Next time, Jord," Harley replied.

"What do you mean, next time?" Enzo asked, out of breath. "I'm not sure if I can do a next time."

She ignored his comment, as she jumped into her car and said,

"Follow me to the graveyard."

 Enzo and Jordan exchanged silent glances, shook their heads, and did as they were told.

XI

After arriving at the graveyard parking lot, Harley stayed in her car, and Jordan and Enzo joined her. Deep inhales overtook the silence between them for a few minutes until she asked, her voice trembling

.

"Is everyone okay? I was terrified for you, Enzo, for all of us." she sighed, looking back at him.

"What the hell happened back there?" he asked. "Was that the Old Hag you spoke about?"

"She explained it all to you earlier," Jordan cut in, "You didn't want to believe her."

"Well, I believe now, even though I couldn't see her, I sure the heck felt her," Enzo said, the tremor in his voice was evident.

"Enzo, if you've decided to step back, I completely understand," Harley offered gently.

"NO!" Jordan shouted, slamming her hands on the dashboard, jolting them. "That's simply not an option; we're in this together."

Harley shot a swift glance at Jordan, then at her rear-view mirror, where Enzo was visibly distressed, rubbing his forehead. His fear was cutting through the silence. Their eyes met for a fleeting moment, and she looked down, her clammy hands twisting together as guilt gnawed at her stomach.

"Why are we even here?" Jordan questioned. "Is it time to retrieve what you need from the grave? Haven't we had enough for one night, Harley?"

"I brought you both here to give you one final opportunity to back out," she replied earnestly. "I hoped that seeing the graves from a distance might make you reconsider."

"I'm still helping," Enzo declared, steeling himself as he opened the door and prepared to jump out. Jordan stayed quiet and followed his lead.

As they marched back to their cars, Harley rolled down her window and called out to Enzo,

 "Be at Jordan's by midnight and rest up. You'll need your strength. This is our last stop before we return to that eerie forest."

The thought of coming back to where it all began made Harley's stomach churn, this graveyard was no sanctuary compared to the Forest of Runes. This was going to be anything but quick and easy.

Jordan shouted back as she swung open her car door,

"I don't think I can sleep; my adrenaline is still racing!"

"Same here," Enzo agreed, slamming his door, he rolled down the window.

"Listen to me," Harley urged. "You need to rest and meet us at Jordan's by midnight—no later, Enzo, or I'll have no choice but to leave you behind."

"Alright, I got it," he nodded, before speeding off.

Once the girls arrived home, they made a beeline for the kitchen to grab a water bottle and then headed straight to their rooms, trying to push aside the haunting memories of the night.

"Get some sleep Jord"

"Glad to," she replied, exhausted, and slammed her bedroom door. Harley retreated to her own room, where she laid in her bed thinking of the night's events until she drifted into her dreams.

A few hours later, Harley shook her friend awake.

"*What…?*" Jordan mumbled.

"We have to leave!" she insisted, and Jordan groaned,

"But I'm still so tired," tossing her blankets aside.

"Put on something old," Harley instructed, ignoring her complaint.

"Why?" Jordan asked, still half-asleep.

 "Because we're going to get a bit dirty."

"Alright, I'm coming," Jordan replied with newfound determination, pulling herself up. "I'll meet you downstairs in a minute."

Before long, both girls stood at the side entrance, geared up in black jogging suits. They laced up their running shoes and went out to the garage.

"By the way, your mom left some food on the warmer for us, Jord. She`s going to start noticing we are not eating? That could raise questions," Harley remarked, with a hint of concern in her voice.

"Don't worry about it; give me a sec," Jordan ran back in a returned with a container of food.

I`m not hungry, Harley stated.

It`s not for us, Jordan said, smiling, I`m giving it to Enzo.

Good call, she smirked, while opening the vehicle door

When they got to the car, she put her key in the ignition and then turned to Jordan; "remember when I said there was one last thing we had to do?"

"Yes, what is it?" Jordan asked, sounding nervous.

"It's about what we needed from the grave." Harley took a big breath, "I was hoping we didn`t need to visit the gravesite."

 "And…?" Jordan pressed, urgency lacing her voice, when a beam of headlights flooded the garage, cutting through the darkness.

"Enzo is waiting outside. I'll fill you in on the way," Harley replied.

"Yeah, I've heard that before Harley," Jordan stated boldly, before she motioned him to park his car in the garage, where they all jumped into Harley's.

As she started to drive away, Enzo spoke up as Jordan passed him the food.

"Anyone grab the shovel?"

"Damn it," Harley whispered, as she reversed into Jordan's driveway.

Jordan swiftly jumped out and dashed to the side entrance, grabbing the small shovel from the bushes.

Enzo ate and the girls stayed quiet during the drive. Once they parked in the graveyard lot, Harley warned,

"An old keeper will probably be lurking around. Stay alert; I don't trust him."

 "I'm really scared," Jordan admitted, her voice trembling. "I hate graveyards."

"Then you can stay here," Enzo blurted.

Jordan shot him an irritated look.

"*Are you serious*? There's a crazy old man on the loose at this hour! I'm not going to sit in the car alone. I'm coming," she said.

Harley cut in, "that's exactly what I need, you with me, Jord. I'll explain everything when we get to the site. Let's go," directing them as they exited the car.

"It's gated," Enzo pointed out, scanning their surroundings. "How do we get in?"

"Follow me," Harley said, and gestured for them to come closer.

They moved quietly until they arrived at a lower-level tunnel hidden along the far left of the wall.

Harley paused; her expression somber as she looked at the entrance.

"It has a small fence over it, but Tess and I managed to pull it open wide enough to climb through."

Jordan squeezed her hand gently.

"We all miss her."

Harley sensed that Jordan felt the weight of Tess's loss deeply because of her caring nature, though she struggled to believe that Jordan would truly mourn her absence.

"I know, I just can't get over the memories of that dreadful night," Harley whispered, as she tried to pull the fencing. "Shoot, it's tougher than I remember."

Enzo jumped beside her, grabbed at it and tore it off. "Shit, sorry," he said as both girls stared at him, stunned and wide-eyed.

"Bloody hell, Enzo, you didn't have to damage it completely," Jordan said, shaking her head as she grabbed her phone for more light.

"I opened it for ya, didn`t I?" Enzo asked, sarcastically, winking at her. "Come on, Jord, be a sport; you go first?" he said, jokingly.

Jordan unleashed a brutal punch to his gut, and he let out a loud cough, followed by a moan.

"Go on, tough guy," she teased back with a smirk. "Or maybe you're not so tough?"

"Seriously, are you two ever going to get along?" Harley shot, boldly. "I'll take the lead; I know exactly where the grave is," a sense of determination in her voice. "See you on the other side."

"Other side of what?" Jordan muttered, "*the tunnel or Hell…?*"

Harley took a moment to glance back at them, seeking reassurance, and noticed Jordan's pallor face; she looked like she might faint.

"I'm really not feeling great," Jordan confessed.

"Say hello to the grave keeper," Enzo chimed in with a hint of irony, pushing her aside as he followed Harley into the tunnel, leaving Jordan behind.

Fearful of the old man, Jordan quickly gathered her strength and trailed after them.

"We're almost there," Harley reassured them, holding her phone light up. "Just a few tight spots ahead."

"It reeks down here," Jordan complained, trying to shield her nose with her sweater. "My shoes are soaked! You didn't mention we'd be trudging through the sewers."

"We're almost through," Harley insisted.

"It's not a sewer, Jordan; it's just some smelly rainwater," Enzo clarified, and then joked. "I've got your back, climb on if you need to."

Jordan rolled her eyes. "Yeah, right! The last time you offered help, Harley ended up flat on her butt."

"You're such a baby," Enzo teased.

"No, I'm not, I`d rather walk," she shot back.

"Stop you guys," Harley demanded; the old man will hear us."

 As they wedged through the last narrow opening, Harley could see a small light.

"*Shhh...*, get down and be quiet." They all slumped down and turned their phones off.

"What do you see?" Enzo whispered.

"I think it's him," she answered. "We'll have to wait a few minutes until he leaves."

Enzo attempted to place the shovel down gently, but it clanked against the metal wall, sending a sharp ping echoing through the tunnel.

"Enzo," Jordan hissed urgently, as the reverberation rang painfully in their ears.

 A haunting voice yelled,

"Who's in there?"

They crouched low. Jordan caught a glimpse of Harley, her hand over her mouth to muffle her fear as she tried not to scream. Enzo remained frozen in place, his heavy breaths resonating against the cold grey structure surrounding him. Jordan could feel Harley's violent tremble against her back, followed by rapid breaths.

Overcome by claustrophobia herself, but desperate to support her friend, Jordan took a steadying breath and whispered,

"Please don't panic now, Harley; I'm not exactly in the best shape myself. Try to stay calm," Jordan pleaded.

"Deep slow breaths, Harley," Enzo urged softly, repeating the phrase until her panting subsided.

Relief washed over Jordan, , she relaxed and rested her hands on her knees.

"Come on, you're always scared, kitten," Enzo teased her, rubbing Jordans' lower back, trying to lighten the mood.

"This is not the time for jokes," she fired back.

Standing up, Harley said, resolutely,

"Alright, let's get out of here before I hyperventilate again. I think he's gone."

"You think? that's comforting, Harley" Jordan replied, her sarcasm masking her own anxiety.

As they emerged from the tunnel, Harley's eyes darted around for the old keeper before she pointed to a large tomb in the distance.

"There," she said, "the one with the lit cross on top. It's right over there."

With perseverance, she led the way, carefully navigating around fresh and old graves, each step a reminder of her last visit.

Branches cracked below their feet, making Jordan jump often,

"Nope, I will never get used to a graveyard and don't want to be buried in one either."

Harley turned and looked at her, surprised.

"Well, I hate to break it to you, Jord, but you will be; we all will.

"Okay, girls, morbid convo, let's change the subject," Enzo interrupted.

Harley grinned.

"This is not funny, I won't be buried here. I refuse," Jordan argued.

Harley came to a sudden halt, ignoring Jordan's last comment,

 "There it is, that's the one, she whispered, and then gagged and bent over to vomit, from a flashback of Tess`s mutilated body, particularly, her dangling eyeball.

 Jordan and Enzo gagged at the same time, and backed away from the lingering smell coming from her.

"My god, Harley, what did you eat?" Jordan asked, boldly.

"Jord…, have some feelings." Enzo snapped.

Jordan blushed,

"I'm sorry. It caught me off guard," she said, lowering her head and tucking her hair behind her ears.

Harley knew Jordan wouldn`t be that rude under normal circumstances and brushed it off.

Enzo pushed Jordan out of the way and rushed to Harley's side, rubbing her back softly. Jordan watched with a hint of humility and punctured the watery gravel with her shoe.

Harley stood up and gently pushed Enzo's arm away,

"Let's go," she said, wiping her mouth. "It's okay Jord," she reassured her friend, knowing what was yet to come.

Shortly after, Harley found herself once again, standing at the grave of Philomena Burton, her grandmother, thought to be the last victim of the Old Hag and turned to Enzo.

"We'll keep watch while you dig," she said. And without hesitation, he started his macabre deed.

Every so often, Jordan glanced at Enzo and asked,

"How's it going?"

Enzo, now annoyed,

"You wanna take over?" he asked, frustrated, as he wiped his forehead.

"No thanks," she replied, "I'm keeping watch."

"Actually…," Harley interjected, turning to Jordan. She held her flashlight between them, illuminating Jordan's frightened face while fearing she might back out. "Remember I told you I'd explain your task here?"

"Yes," Jordan replied.

"This won`t be easy, Jord; I know, I couldn't even do it. Heck, Enzo couldn't even do it," she pointed out.

"You're freaking me out now," Jordan whispered. "Just say it, tell me what I need to do?" her voice steady.

"Well..."

As Harley began to speak, a loud bang came from the grave, causing both girls to look down in shock.

"Already..." Jordan shrieked, her eyes wide.

"Yup," Enzo answered as he started to pull himself up and off the exposed coffin.

"Well, stay there. You need to open it, Enzo," Jordan ordered. "We can't lift that lid; it's too heavy," not admitting she didn`t want to see inside.

Enzo let himself go, sliding back onto the coffin and started to pry the shovel into it. The girls watched until he began to lift the top slowly. Jordan quickly turned her head away and clenched her eyes.

Enzo jumped out, and Harley just stared at what was left of her grandmother's face—a dark creviced face stared back with one eye, while the other was now home to piles of slithering maggots. Jordan peeked over and turned quickly, covering her mouth.

Enzo asked, "Why does the body still have so much flesh if this is an old ancestor?

Harley stood violently shaking, and started to cry, dropping to her knees, she put her hands over her face.

"Look again, Enzo". she said.

He took his phone light and directed its beam closer to the body. The sight made him instinctively recoil, his heart racing as he stumbled over a flowerpot while backing away, a somber tribute left for another.

Jordan watched Enzo; fear etched on her face.

"What did you see?" Jordan demanded, concern in her voice.

"This is the wrong site, Jordan," Harley quickly interjected, her tone grave. "Turn away Jord," she urged, but Jordan couldn't resist. She pointed her light towards the grave.

Enzo sprang into action, swiftly covering Jordan's mouth to muffle her on-coming scream.

"*Shhh*…," he whispered, pulling her close. "You will wake the grave keeper."

Some time had passed and gradually, Enzo felt Jordan's body loosen, and he slowly removed his hand.

Jordan hesitantly glanced back at the grave, pointing with trembling hands.

"It doesn't look like Tess, something isn't right," she said, crying. "She's... mangled! and where is her eye?"

"It's her," Harley whispered, sadly, "but I don`t understand why I was drawn to this site, and why it's marked Philomena Burton. We have to find my grandmother. There's something deeply sinister at play here— This is a horrible warning of what could happen if we don't stop that Witch—especially for me," Harley admitted, her face pale while she scanned the area. "The site is close; I know it," she insisted, pointing ahead. "Just a little further maybe."

"Are you absolutely sure this time?" Enzo asked, stretching his sore arms.

"I'll help you; we can take turns," she replied, wiping away her tears, resolve replacing her fear.

A few minutes later, Jordan stood in silence, frozen by the weight of the moment as Harley and Enzo took turns digging a second grave, they found marked with the same name, Philomena Burton. Thoughts of escape flashed through her mind, but she couldn't bring herself to move.

With one final stroke of the shovel, a coffin broke free from the earth beneath them. Enzo pried open the lid, and this time, stared quietly in disbelief at the corpse that lay within.

"I would have thought your grandmother would have rotted more," Jordan blurted, breaking the silence.

"*Jord*...," Enzo angered, glaring at her, "what's wrong with you? That's her family that lay there."

"Shut it, Enzo," Jordan snapped back, sternly. "It's my nerves. Look what we are doing here; this is unreal. I think empathy is overrated at this point."

Enzo put his arm around Harley`s waist.

"I'm fine," she said, quietly, staring down at her grandmother's pale, partially wrinkled face, she could see a resemblance to the portrait in the attic, but didn`t share her thoughts. "I never knew her."

"Do you think the curse prevented her from rotting?, or maybe you're good witch ancestry?" Jordan asked, her tone direct.

Harley and Enzo exchanged concerned glances. Enzo shook his head, disturbed, while Harley chose to overlook Jordan's bluntness once more.

Just as Harley was about to explain what lay ahead, she turned to Jordan and whispered,

"Are you ready?" and rolled up the leg of her track pants revealing a formidable knife.

"Whoa!" Enzo exclaimed, leaning in closer. "You had that with you the whole time?"

Without replying, Harley smoothly extracted the blade from its holder.

"Damn, Harley, that's a butcher's knife," Enzo remarked, surprise etched on his face.

"Exactly what we need," she shot back, her gaze fierce.

"What do we need it for?" Jordan asked, her voice trembling.

She could see Jordan's anxiety manifesting quickly.

"There's something I haven't told you, Jord. The letter Tess found also detailed what I need from the grave and clearly states that it has to be a non-cursed female to retrieve it, I can`t explain why. But for now, you're the only non-cursed female. I need the hands of the last ancestor killed."

Jordan took a step back, eyes wide, and cried out,

 "No way! Are you really asking me to do that? She pointed at the lifeless woman, petrified by the request. "No way, Harley! Absolutely not. You're losing it! I can`t believe you dragged me out here to do this without first telling me.

"*Shhh…*" Enzo interjected quietly. "We don't have time for this, Jord. Daylight is approaching, and we need to leave the graveyard soon, before the Keeper makes his appearance again. Please, you have to do this," he pleaded, desperation in his voice. Think about Harley and Tess.

"You do it then, Enzo," she argued.

"He can't. It has to be you, Jord, and I promise I will read you the letter as soon as we get out of here," Harley pleaded, wedging the knife between Jordan's delicate hands.

Enzo watched the knife shake as she held it; all Jordan could do was stare at it.

"Here, let me help you," Enzo said, as he took the knife and gently guided her closer to the grave and slowly lowered her down before handing the knife back.

Harley watched Jordan closely; she looked lost and fragile while standing there alone and afraid. Jordan kneeled, crying, looked up to the heavens, and said,

"Forgive me, Father," as she started cutting into the first wrist. She gagged with every slice and crack of a bone. Enzo ran, leaned on the next grave, and heaved.

She just kept watch as Jordan completed the gory deed.

"Get me out of here!" Jordan cried after dropping the knife when she was done.

Harley jumped in and grabbed a bag stashed in her hoodie pocket, "Just put them in here, Jord," she said, holding the bag open.

"Haven't I done enough?" Jordan asked, boldly.

"I can't touch them," Harley replied, as she grabbed the soiled knife and stuck it back in it's holder.

 Enzo hurried back to the site and helped the girls out. "Let's get out of here now," he demanded.

"Wait," Jordan said. "What about Tess? How is she even there?"

"I'm not sure," Harley replied, "There's nothing we can do about her right now."

"Yeah, she can't come with us, Jordan," Enzo said, spitting on the ground and then grabbed the shovel.

Jordan looked at him,

"You're sick," she replied.

"Would you two stop bickering and let's get going?" Harley whispered.

As they approached the tunnel, the old man suddenly leaped out, causing them all to fall to the ground.

"What are you doing here?" he shouted at them and staggered forward.

Harley jumped to her feet.

"We came to leave some flowers for my grandmother," she said, relieved he didn`t notice the shovel Enzo tucked behind his back.

"You! You're that same girl from before, the one with the card and the invisible friend," the old keeper laughed.

Harley wasn't amused.

"Yeah, that was me, old man, and I saw my friend; it was you," she yelled, backing up.

Enzo and Jordan quickly followed suit.

"You killed Tess," she accused, moving to the right in an attempt to escape. "I have proof."

The old man followed her, turning in her direction. "There you go again, girl, you and your make-believe stories," he scowled.

While **Harley** argued with the old keeper, Enzo quietly crept up behind him, grasping the shovel tight. Just as he was about to hit the man with it, some invisible force, surprised him, yanking it from his hand and sent it flying into the air. Enzo ran to retrieve it, but the old keeper shouted at him,

"Leave it alone, lad"

Harley watched as the man's face started to twist in an unsettling manner.

Jordan rubbed her eyes to get clear look. Harley knew Jordan was seeing what she was seeing; the old keeper was being controlled by something and began to walk toward Enzo.

"Get away from him!" Harley yelled. She ran to Enzo, "Leave him alone; jumping in front, "it's me, you want. Enzo, run. *NOW*," she ordered.

Enzo ran toward the tunnel, where Jordan was already waiting. He grabbed Jordan's hand.

"Let's go," he whispered, looking back at Harley. "She'll be okay," Enzo said, "She knows what she's doing. She has a plan, right?"

Jordan shook her head,

"I hope so." Dismissing the whole "we`re in this together phrase" she quickly followed him in, leaving Harley behind.

Harley held the bagged hands tightly behind her back, convinced that this was what the keeper was after, to prevent her from breaking the curse. It was clear to her that the man before her was not the same one from that morning; he was being manipulated by something unseen.

In a sudden movement, he lunged toward her, but she swiftly ducked to the side, seizing the opportunity to escape. Echoes of squeals, burrowed deep within her eardrums again. As Harley ran toward the tunnel, she could hear the old man`s stomping feet closing in behind.

But as she approached the opening, it became instantly quiet. She looked back again just in time to see him fall, and without a second thought, she turned, dropped to her knees and crawled into the tunnel.

Relieved, Jordan hugged her, feeling a pinch of guilt. "You're safe!"

"Listen to me," Harley insisted, pushing the bag toward Jordan. "Take this and go ahead. Remember, no one but you can touch those hands."

"What?" Enzo questioned. "You're coming with us, right?"

"I'll only be a couple of minutes behind. I need to see something first."

"Please, don't do this. Come with us!" Jordan pleaded, desperation lacing her words.

"I promise, no danger, she assured them; it's just a minute, go now; I will meet you at the car," she ordered.

As she peaked out of the Tunnel, she heard a low groan from the yard; she watched the man sit up and shake his head; as he slowly stood, he looked unsteady, "Maybe he`s drunk," she thought.

But then it appeared, hovering above him, was a grey mist,

"No Way!" she whispered, as she watched in shock. A glimpse of the woman's face protruded and then receded quickly.

The man fell back and then looked up, but as he turned and tried to crawl away, he was lifted from his knees and thrown, landing in a sitting position against a tomb; he moaned in pain.

Her eyes widened, as he started yelling for help. Harley wanted to run to him but couldn't move; all she could do was watch. And then she saw it rise into the air...

"*Nooo*!" she screamed silently in shock. "*Nooo*!" tears falling from her cheeks. Her stomach twisted with guilt as she did nothing but watch the shovel lunge into the man's neck- the same shovel they used to dig up Philomena Burton's hands, and Tess.

She turned her head quickly and cupped her mouth, trying to stop her scream, and when all became silent, she looked back, peering out the edge of the Tunnel again, watching as the face of the Old Hag disappear back into her doomy mist. Harley turned and crawled through the Tunnel as fast as her trembling body would allow.

She caught up with Enzo and Jordan, where both greeted her with a hug, glad she was safe. They hustled through the rest of the tunnel, made their way to their vehicles, leaving the graveyard behind.

XII

Her phone buzzed in her pocket, prompting Harley to turn on the night lamp beside her bed. She was surprised to see the Bayview Library's number on her screen.

Oh no, the librarian knows I took the book.

She quickly hit the hang-up button, silenced her notifications, and placed the phone on the nightstand, forgetting to turn off vibrate mode.

BUZZZ—it started vibrating again. Startled, she grabbed the phone to hang up, but her instincts told her to answer. Peeking over to make sure she didn't wake Jordan, she said.

"Hello."

"Hello Harley, is this you?" the lady on the phone asked.

"Yes, it's me."

"Oh, I am so happy, you answered, It's me, the librarian from Bayview, do you remember me?"

"Yes," she replied.

"I need to see you, I need to talk to you."

"About what?" Harley asked, concerned.

"It's about why you entered the attic," the librarian whispered.

Harley gulped hard.

"You know I took the book?"

"Yes, I know about the book, that book is useless now," the librarian replied.

Harley was quiet for a minute and then asked sternly,

"Useless, how would you know this or what I might need it for?"

"You must meet me, Harley, she said, ignoring her questions, please meet me in my office at 7am this morning; I can help you, that's all I will say for now, goodbye."

The woman hung the phone up in her ear. Concerned but tired, Harley laid back, staring at her phone screen, wondering why this woman wanted to see her or what she thought she knew. She pulled her cell back and set her alarm for six a.m.

"An hour and a half, ugh," she said, rolling over. Pulling the covers over her head, she drifted into her dreams again.

A while later, Jordan woke up, hearing loud music coming from her friends cell, she jumped out of bed, stubbing her toe on the night table,

"Ouch," she screeched. "Harley, your alarm," she said, as she limped over.

Harley could feel her body gently shaking, and slowly opened her eyes, a burning sensation flushing through as she rubbed them.

"What Jord," she asked, disoriented.

"Your alarm, why do you set it so early?"

"Oh, that," she replied, more awake, "I have to be somewhere."

"Where are you going now?"

"I received a weird call from the librarian after you fell asleep. She knows about the book."

"Oh no, how much trouble are you in?" Jordan asked, sitting on the bed, rubbing her foot.

"None," she said. "the librarian actually said something about helping me. It wasn't making sense, so I'm going to meet her. I will know more later."

"Okay, I'm going back to bed," Jordan said, as she stood up.

"Yes, rest more, Jordan, we have a big night ahead."

Hopping back in bed, Jordan put her pillow over her head, not wanting to be reminded.

Harley grabbed what she needed for her shower and left the room. Once ready, she hurried downstairs, made a coffee and a quick bite to eat, and sat at the kitchen table.

As, she bit a piece of toast, she wondered,

Maybe this is a trick, I am in trouble, or perhaps the librarian does know something more?

"Good morning, Harley." Jordan's mom said.

Startled, she spilled some coffee on her shirt,

"*Shit*," she whispered.

"Pardon," Jan asked, smirking.

"Oh, it's nothing, Jan, I just spilled a bit of coffee on my shirt, but yes, good morning," Harley replied, as she stuffed the book away.

"Nothing dry cleaning can't fix," Jan stated, warmly "You're up early; where's my daughter?"

"Getting her beauty sleep," Harley joked.

Jordan's mom chuckled.

"I'm heading off to work now. I truly hope to see you both for supper tonight! It feels like I hardly see you ladies anymore; you're always on the go."

"I'll be sure to tell Jordan." Harley replied, as Jan started to leave. "Have a wonderful day, Jan!"

Harley quickly changed her shirt and grabbed her keys, eager to make her way to the library. Once there, she knocked lightly on the librarian's door and heard a cheerful voice call out,

"Come in!"

As Harley opened the door, the librarian was sitting cross-legged on the floor, with her arms half extended.

"A yoga pose, maybe," she thought, intrigued.

"Ah, I'm so glad you're here!" jumping to her feet. "I have some exciting news!"

"What's so important?" Harley asked, hesitantly.

"Please, sit," the woman said eagerly, gesturing towards a cozy two-seat leather couch. "Make yourself comfortable, Harley.

As Harley settled in, her eyes wandered around the room, landing on small containers arranged neatly on the desk and a nearby side table.

Is that salt? she wondered, interested.

The librarian turned to her and asked,

"Can I have the book, please?" extending her delicate hand out, expectantly.

As Harley passed her the book, she recognized a beautiful vintage stone glistening from around the woman's neck.

"That's a very nice necklace," she said, thinking of her own gem collection packed away.

 "Thank you," the librarian replied with a gentle touch to the stone, "It`s Garnet."

Harley shook her head, agreeing silently.

"Now, first of all, I didn`t formally introduce myself correctly last time. **My name is Mary, the head librarian.**

She observed as Mary gently placed the book into a box on a shelf, retrieved a key from her jacket hanging on her desk chair, and locked it away.

"Why is this book so important if it's so useless?" Harley inquired.

"I suppose I should have explained it differently," Mary replied. "It`s useless to you now, but it could hold great value for someone else's research in the future."

"What do you really know about me and my interests?" Harley pressed, a hint of defensiveness in her tone.

Mary took a seat beside her.

"Can I get you something to drink? Water, coffee? Perhaps a snack?" Mary gently rubbed Harley's arm. "There are fresh apples and pears on my desk."

She glanced at Mary's hand on hers, then quickly pulled away, feeling uncomfortable.

"What do you need to tell me, Mary?" She asked, impatiently.

"Here, this is for you," Mary said, handing an envelope over. "Please don't open it yet; I would like to tell you a story first."

"What story?" she asked, curiously.

Taking no time, Mary blurted out, "I know about the sinister woman."

"What woman?" Harley responded, creasing her brows.

"I know about all of it because my mother is the reason for this nightmare" Mary stated.

She slowly sat back on the couch, her expression softening as Mary replayed the tragic night of her mother.

"The ritual my mother performed, caused a curse that claimed her life; the Old Hag was able to get to her, and sadly, my mother was killed. Harley, our family was protected for a very long time until…" she said, lowering her gaze as a tear slipped down her cheek.

"How does this involve me?" Harley asked, emotions cold while frustration boiled. "That's your family's issue, not mine," she stated, rising from her seat.

"I understand," Mary replied, her voice heavy with empathy. "But thinking about my mother fills me with sorrow. It's incredibly painful when a mother and daughter are torn apart."

"Yes, I know very well;" Harley replied, boldly, and stood to leave, "I lost mine too."

Mary looked up at her; "I know you did; she agreed; I know a lot about you and your family, more than you think."

"Okay, I`m leaving now," Harley said and waved her hand, not wanting to hear anymore, "you have your book."

Mary leaped up; her voice urgent.

"Wait!" she shouted.

Harley halted, her gaze fixated on the office door, desperate to escape.

"Please, just wait," Mary pressed. "Did you dig up the grave?"

She squeezed her eyes shut, taking a deep breath before turning and confronting Mary.

"What did you just ask me?" She retorted, slowly advancing toward her. "That's some disturbing accusation."

Mary's tone turned serious,

"*Shhh...*, keep it down," she insisted.

Panic quickly filled, as Harley thought this woman was making up stories to make her talk about the gravesite,

Maybe she is working with the authorities?

Now extremely worried the Librarian may call the police, a dark notion of violence briefly flared in Harley's mind. She shook it off quickly.

"Please believe me, Harley, I also know that tarot cards and a Ouija planchette were used in the conjuring process," Mary declared. And, I'm the one that has been leaving the tarot cards for you, only to let you know, that you were on the right path."

Harley felt a stab to the chest.

"So, you were there when Tess was killed? *What did you do to her*?" The fury in her voice was unmistakable.

"I swear, I didn't see anything, Mary admitted. I went to the gravesite because it was the anniversary of my mother's death. When I arrived at the site, I found you passed out and alone. I tried to help you, but the groundskeeper showed up. I had no choice but to flee."

The librarian continued to speak softly,

"I understand this deadly curse; it affects every third generation. I know everything," Mary assured her, her eyes earnest. "Those Tarot cards were meant to show you that you are on the right path, Harley. You need to listen to me, you have the power to reverse this curse. I also know where you were born," Mary declared, what day it was, and even the exact time."

Harley's jaw dropped, and she sank deep, back into her seat, utterly numb.

"I know this is an overwhelming revelation, but there's so much more," Mary continued, locking eyes with her. "I`m also aware that your mom tragically passed away in a fire at work not long ago and you father left. But you need to understand this: I will always be here for you," she said with kindness.

Harley, snapped, fueled by anger and grief, firing back,

"*How dare you bring my parents into this? You never knew them*!"

"Actually, I did know them, Harley. I met them years ago, when I made a heart-wrenching decision...," Mary hesitated for a brief moment, "I gave you to them!"

"What? You must be out of your mind! And I'm out of here," she shouted, springing to her feet and bolted for the door.

"*Stop, please*! You need to understand!" Mary begged, her voice rising with desperation. "I had to give you up, to protect you from the curse that haunts our family. I believed if you were hidden, the ties severed, then you would be safe. I've endured unimaginable pain, and I still do. But when you walked in here, and, after seeing you at the gravesite, I recognized the very thing you were searching for, I realized that the Old Hag—the curse—it found you. And I was certain at that moment I did too, I knew then that you would need help from a living ancestor and that you had become tangled in this dark fate."

Without looking back, Harley opened the door, sensing Mary's presence behind her.

"Please, take this," Mary said, unhooking her necklace. "I know you're angry with me now, and rightly so. This is a lot to absorb," she admitted, her voice softening. "But everything you need to understand is in that envelope. Please, for your safety."

Mary placed the necklace in Harley's hand, along side the envelope.

"This is for protection."

Harley remained silent, feeling empty. She stared at the garnet pendant that dangled from her fingers and walked out of the office, slamming the door with a resonating finality.

XIII

Sitting in her car, overwhelmed, Harley stared at herself in the rear view mirror. She cried, leaning her forehead on the steering wheel, struggling to process the news. After wiping her eyes again, she started driving to Jordan's. Putting her car in park, she could hear Jordan's mom yelling inside the house and rushed in quickly.

"What's wrong?" she shouted, entering the kitchen.

Jordan and her mom turned to face her.

"Harley," Jordan blurted, I`m sorry, her eyes motioning at the item her mom held.

Miss Bozzelli looked at her and demanded,

"*What is this?*"

Harley walked up to Jan and took the tarot card from her hand.

"It's a tarot card, Jan," she said, lowering her gaze.

"What have I told you ladies about using those evil objects in this house?" Miss Bozzelli scolded.

"I'm so sorry," she replied, giving Jordan a look to intervene.

"Mom, I explained that we found it, no disrespect, we wouldn`t use them in here."

"I was going to get rid of it," Harley quickly lied, when suddenly, a thought struck her, and her heart raced as she recalled the hands in the shrubs. "Jord told me to throw it away, but I forgot, Jan. I promise, this is not Jordan's fault."

Jordan`s mom paused calmly, staring at the them with a serious expression.

The room became extremely uncomfortable,

Jan didn`t get upset often, but when she did, you wanted to run.

Harley looked over at Jordan whose was face flushed.

Jan finally spoke, "I'm pretty easy-going, don't you both think? You eat good food, drink great wine, I don`t usually mingle."

Both Harley and Jordan nodded, embarrassed.

"Well, all I ask that you don't bring anything evil into my house."

Harley swallowed hard. "No, never again, Miss Bozzelli. I will get rid of it now."

She turned toward the patio door, pretending to dispose of the card and quickly checked the shrubs, relieved; the hands were still there. She slipped the tarot card into her back pocket and thought.

What if Jan found my grandmothers hands?

Knowing how angry Jords mom was, as she didn't correct her when she addressed her as Miss Bozzelli, Harley shook her head, disgusted at the thought.

 Not long after, Jordan rushed outside.

"Harley, we need to grab the other card from my closet before my mom finds them; she's always snooping."

"I realized that, Jord," she replied. "We have a worse problem: I don't have the book with the reversal curse; I gave it back before tearing out the page first."

"*What*? We need that. It's the most important part!" Jordan exclaimed anxiously.

"You keep your mom occupied for a few minutes while I run upstairs to grab the cards, and then I'll figure something out," Harley suggested. "I also have something to show you," she added, as they returned inside.

Jordan dashed to distract her mother in the dining room while she hurried to retrieve the rest of the cards. Jan left for work shortly after, and both girls sat in their usual spot on the patio.

"What did you want to show me?" Jordan asked.

Harley threw an envelope onto the table.

"What's this?" Jordan asked, curiously, picking it up.

"I'm not sure, I haven't opened it yet."

Her answer left Jordan looking confused,

"OK, I wonder if it has anything to do with tonight?"

Harley, didn't respond to her question, instead, she began recounting her meeting with the librarian.

"She knew everything, Jord, and then she gave me this necklace, said it was for protection," and then, Harley said, tapping the envelope, she handed me this."

"Is this woman mad?" Jordan questioned. "How could she know anything about you, Harley? Stay away from her, and I'll throw this envelope away right now." Jordan stood, reaching for it.

Harley grabbed her wrist to stop her.

"Maybe I should just see what's inside," she said, apprehensively.

Jordan felt her hand tremble.

"It will be fine," Jordan reassured her while carefully removing some papers from the envelope.

A picture fell onto the table, followed by another familiar object. Harley picked up the image of a woman and a baby. The woman resembled Mary , causing her heart to ache, and a tear rolled down her cheek.

Jordan stood to comfort her.

"It's OK, giving her a tight squeeze. I will help you get through this," she promised, then returned to the envelope, picking up another object. "Oh crap," Jordan exclaimed, tossing it into her lap. "Sorry," she added, intending to throw it onto the table. "I got a little freaked out."

Harley studied it,

Another tarot card—identical to the last.

"What is with these cards?" Jordan asked.

"Mary, said they were to indicate that I was on the right track. Maybe they were used during the ritual," Harley replied, turning the card over; there was tiny scribbling. "What's this?" She whispered as she inspected it closely.

Jordan ripped it from her hand.

"It reads, continue to be brave…, ok, that makes no sense," Jordan said, dropping it on the table and then carefully slid another paper from the envelope. Her eyes widened, as she handed it to Harley. Stunned by what she quickly scanned.

"It's true," Harley stated, after careful investigation. "It's a copy of my birth record, stating Mary Burton as my birth parent; no father is known." Harley banged the table with her fist. "Why didn't my parents tell me?" she asked, demanding an answer. Why would they leave me with this, Jord?

 Jordan leaned back in her chair, worried at what other reaction her friend may have.

"Calm down; I know it's overwhelming; you need time, Harley," and hesitated to point something else out. "Don`t freak out but look at your birth date, according to that record, you turned 20, four months ago!"

"*What*?" Harley inhaled deeply when her friends words really resonated and then exclaimed, "I knew it, this does have something to do with my age." She twirled her finger in a strand of hair. "I don't have time, Jord; I will end up like my grandmother."

Jordan felt a knot form in her stomach. She sat quietly while Harley continued,

"My grandmother was the last ancestor murdered by the cursed Old Hag, and we don't even have the spell now, Jord," she said.

Jordan looked again at the envelope.

"There is one more piece of paper to pull out. Do you want me to do it, or do you want to?" Jordan asked, anxiously.

"I don't think I can handle any more information," Harley stated, as she pushed the envelope toward her friend.

"OK, let's see," Jordan said, pulling out the last paper carefully.

Skimming through the first section of the document, Harley sat with anticipation, holding her breath until Jordan jumped up excitedly.

 "What is it, Jord?" she asked, with a long exhale.

Jordan smirked and started waving the paper in the air, jumping up and down like a child with candy.

"What?" Harley asked again.

Jordan stopped dancing around the kitchen island to read it.

 "It's the reversal curse," she said, smiling. "It says we need to enter the Old Hag's den with an item of protection, the hand bones of the last ancestor killed. It also says that you need to step into the center of thirteen runes."

Harley sighed loudly, and stopped twirling her hair,

"Good thing we kept them and threw them in Enzos trunk," she replied."

A minute later, Jordan started to read the second section; her excitement diminished, and she slammed the paper on the table.

Harley, now concerned, leaned over to read the rest,

"Enter the Den through the back door and perform this spell, toss everything into the boiling water, and then drink from the spoon that stirred the pot. Any person performing the ritual with you, must also drink from the pot; once done, hold hands and repeat this saying thirteen times, this is the number of the witch, do this at exactly1500 hrs. Then exit through the front door."

"Omg, I'm going to pass out," Jordan said, dramatically, "this is too much," and sat back down, her leg bouncing from anxiety. "I can't do it, Harley. Boiled flesh and bones, your grandmother's hands, she said, disgustingly, and possibly old blood on those bones, gross. I can't," she repeated, shaking her head, "I can't drink blood," heaving at the thought.

"Then stay here," Harley replied. "I can do this on my own."

Jordan jumped up from her seat again and started pacing back and forth, biting her fingernails while she listened to her, quietly deliberating with herself.

"Dammit, Jordan finally shouted, I'm coming; if I pass out, make Enzo carry me out and never forget what I am doing for you," she demanded, as she pointed at her.

"Great," Harley replied, as she ran over to hug her. "It's late now, let's grab everything, including Enzo, and get going."

When the girls pulled into Enzo's driveway, he was nowhere to be seen.

"Text him, Jordan; he might be sleeping."

Jordan did as she was told, and a few minutes later, Enzo jumped into the back seat, scaring them; both girls turning to look at him.

"What," he asked, shrugging, innocently.

"Geez, Enzo, always a surprising entrance," Jordan complained, and then she turned back to Harley, whispering. "Don't say anything to him yet, we need him; he's strong; but he might run."

"I doubt that, Jord," she argued, quietly. "Do you not remember him being pinned down?" that should have scared him away, but he's still coming with us."

Looking back at Enzo, "are you ready for this?" Jordan asked.

"More than ready," he said, and punched his arm, as though he heard what they had said.

Jordan shook her head and rolled her eyes, "*whatever*," she replied, turning and settling snugly in the passenger seat.

As they pulled up to the forest, Enzo said, "let's do this *quick*."

 "Of course, Jordan agreed; you're going first," she told Enzo.

"Huh, me? why?"

"Because you're strongest," Harley said with a smirk.

Enzo hopped out of the back seat.

"Fine."

"Yes, please, let's finally end this morbid quest," Jordan replied.

Harley also agreed, slamming the car door and stood beside Jordan. "Be careful guys."

Harley felt more assertive this time as they approached the mouth of the forest, but a slight tremble from Jordan's arm revealed her anxiety.

"It's ok, Jord, we'll do this fast, in and out."

"Wasn't that easy last time," Jordan replied, with uncertainty.

 Walking ahead, Enzo stated,

"At least we're not going in blind this time, Jord." He looked back at her and then jumped quickly to the right, startled by the cracking of the branches below his feet, "watch your step."

Jordan quickly ran to him, "I'll protect you, Enzo," wrapping her arm around his waist and giggling her fear away.

"Haha, funny Jord, that's not cool;" wiggling his waist from her grip, "let me go, geez, your such a child sometimes," he smirked.

Jordan removed her arm, gave him a slight shove on the shoulder, and rolled her eyes.

"Stop you two, look ahead," Harley said, pointing at the creepy cabin.

A light was on in the window again. They crouched and crept cautiously.

As they moved closer, Jordan covered her eyes briefly and then quickly pulled her hands away.

"What the hell? I must be seeing things; it's not windy out. Do you guys see the rocking chair moving?" Jordan asked.

"Yeah, it's like someone is sitting in it," Enzo replied.

Jordan immediately grabbed 'Enzo's hoodie, startling him, making him jump and speak loudly,

"*WHAT?*"

She took a step back, shocked, and responded to his outburst,

"Geez, *are you going to be ok*?" she asked, eye brows creased and hoping for reassurance from him.

"Sorry, Jord, I wish you ladies would stop asking me that, but yeah," he answered uneasily.

"We have to get around the Den to the black door," Harley stated. "I'm worried about what happened last time, Enzo, when you went to the back of this gloomy place."

"I'll be fine in the back," he replied, swiping his unsteady hand over his face "not so sure about the inside though, is there anything else I should be aware of, Harley?

"No questions, Enzo," Jordan piped in, tapping Harley's shoulder, reminding her they shouldn't scare Enzo into running.

"Huh, oh yeah," she agreed. "I have a plan, Enzo."

 Harley looked back at Jordan, with a guilty expression and then down at her cell; 1:45. She whispered,

"We have to hurry."

"We should have brought the lantern," Jordan said.

 "Next time, Jord," Enzo answered, annoyed, narrowing his brows now.

"*What*," Jordan asked, surprised and raising her voice, "there will be no next time, turning to Harley for reassurance."

"You`re so gullible," Jord, Enzo said, laughing.

"He's messing with you, Jordan, he likes igniting your fire. But of course, we are ending this tonight, even if it kills me," and with that said, Harley stuffed her phone in her pocket.

Jordan and Enzo shot her their own look that could kill; she ignored the seriousness in their eyes.

Enzo whispered, pointing to the side of the cabin.

"I took this way," remembering his steps from the last time.

They all edged their backs tightly against the Den and crept quietly along the gnarled ancient logs until they stood staring at the weathered black door.

"Now what?" Jordan whispered.

And Just as she spit the words out, a dark mist circled the three of them and disappeared instantly. They stood silent, staring at the door, too scared to move, waiting for the next bolt from the darkness.

Enzo slowly turned and looked behind at the unearthly tree. He could see the branches starting to sway the same unusual way as last time,

"Here we go," he stated, alerting the girls.

Harley looked back, and then started shoving him.

"Hurry, get inside," she demanded, eagerly, before hearing the loud, familiar squeal in the distance.

"The wicked old Hag is on her way," Jordan kept repeating, "I'm going to lose it," she cried, as she anxiously jumped from one foot to the other.

Enzo quickly grabbed the door handle and started pulling,

"It's not opening," he yelled, over the gusts of wind.

"Pull harder," Harley ordered, but without waiting, she pushed him aside, and slid in front of the door.

Jordan shouted, "What is happening?" pointing at Harley's chest.

Calmness radiated around them momentarily while they gazed at the glowing garnet pendant hanging from her neck. Not giving it another thought, Harley pulled hard on the door handle, which forcefully flew open, sending all of them to the ground.

Jordan screamed in pain, grabbing her side.

"It hurts."

Enzo stood up and tried to run toward her, but an unseen energy was forcing him back; Harley impulsively jumped in front of him and ordered him to stay behind. Relieved the necklace was protecting them, she could move closer to Jordan while keeping Enzo safe.

"Enzo, Hurry, lift Jordan?" Harley said.

He swiftly locked his arm under Jordan's shoulder, as he was told.

"Easy," he said, steadying her as he helped her stand.

She limped beside him as he held her tight.

When they entered the Den, Jordan yelled, forgetting her pain for the minute.

"There it is, Harley, the pot for the fire, exactly what we need.

After quickly scanning the room, Harley started laying out her orders,

"Quick, Enzo, grab the pot and fill it with water."

"The squeals are getting closer, *hurry*, please," Jordan begged.

"You should sit, Jord," Harley suggested as she tossed the bag on the floor next to them; she helped Jordan walk closer to the fire pit and lowered her down gently. "Stay here; don't move."

Jordan did as she was told.

"Bring the pot here, Enzo," pointing to the unlit coals and wood.

Running back with it, Enzo admitted, "It's heavy enough for a small pot," and placed it over the wood, wiping sweat from the back of his neck.

Ignoring his complaint, Harley told him to light a fire as she removed everything but the hands from the bag.

"Hurry, it's even closer," Jordan cried, burying her head in her knees.

"Jord, I do need one last thing from you," she said, calmly, feeling bad for her friend.

"*What now*?" she asked, looking up, frustrated, "I thought you wanted me to stay put?"

Harley walked to her with the black silk bag and dangled it before Jordan's face.

Jordan squinted her nose at her and gave it a slap,

"Sick"; she said.

"You have to, Jord, just grab them fast and toss them into the pot."

"Enzo…, grab these hands and throw them in the pot," Jordan ordered, ignoring Harley.

"Why me?" he argued, "this is your task, Jordan."

"Oh for fuck sake's, Enzo," Jordan replied, boldly, while sticking her shaky hand in the air. "Pass me the bag, Harley, I know it's my job."

Harley's jaw dropped, stunned. She never heard Jordan swear, but she obeyed without delay and lowered the silk bag closer while Enzo shook his head and turned to prepare the fire.

She left Jordan gagging over the hands as she ran back to the pot, tossing everything else in and then quickly laying the thirteen runes around Jordan, leaving just enough room for her and Enzo.

"A foot away from the burning pot, the perfect distance," she thought.

"Enzo," she said, "I need you to...,"

Just as she was about to continue, her words were cut off by a massive bang on the front door.

"Shush," Harley demanded, holding her finger to her mouth, while they stood quietly, staring at the door listening—not a sound but the crackling fire could be herd.

Their eyes slowly scanned the room until a light tapping noise started from above.

Looking up at the ceiling, they feared what was next.

Jordan cupped her ears, rocking back and forth on the floor; looking like a scared child in a dirty playpen,

"Oh hell," she cried, "we're going to die."

Cringing to the sounds of nails digging into the roof above,

"What is that?" Enzo asked.

"*Shhh...*," Harley said to them again, as she kept listening,.

Her eyes continued to follow the prominent, tapping, that soon reduced to redundant scratching and gouging at the old roof until it stopped abruptly. The room went completely silent. They all stayed still while their fear multiplied, itching their skin.

As they scanned the room a bit longer, a loud thud of the back door flying open, scaring them nearly to death. Harley and Enzo quickly jumped back while Jordan was startled so bad, that she threw one of the hands toward the black mist.

"Jordan, *NO*!" Harley yelled, as she reached out.

"I'm sorry," Jordan hollered back, hugging her knees again and wedging her face between, while the other hand dangled from her fingers.

 Harley leaped out of the circle of runes, running to grab the hand, but she was thrown to the ground.

"Har…, Enzo yelled,

"Stay there!" she ordered, as she lay pinned to the floor.

The mist slowly hovered over Harley's limp body. Harley could see a silhouette of an aged, very gruesome face, dark and evil, as it gradually emerged. She fought hard to wiggle away but felt the heavy weight on her chest. Yet somehow she was able to dig her elbows into the brittle floor boards, ignoring every painful splinter, as she slowly edged away.

"Help her, Enzo," Jordan hollered, terrified and crying.

 As horrified as Enzo seemed to be, Harley watched as he jumped in to help her. She as though the Old Hag was sitting on her, only she really wasn't; *what was happening?*

Harley feared this might be it, the moment she would feel the dreadful pain of her fate at the hands of this sadistic evil witch. She stared into her blood red beady eyes until she heard a loud thump; Harley quickly turned her head, and saw Enzo passed out against the wall. She looked back, the Hag started to retreat into her mist, and then it disappeared to a different location of the room.

"*ENZO*," she yelled, sitting up quickly "*LEAVE HIM ALONE, HAG.*"

Jordan watched, scared and confused, as her friend screamed at something unseen in the corner of the room.

Harley swiftly turned onto her hands and knees, eying the area for the hand, she yelled,

"Where did it land, Jord?"

"There," Jordan hollered back, pointing at the gruesome hand.

As Harley struggled to crawl, something grabbed her leg and pulled her back. She flipped herself over, and it let go, again disappearing. *She's taunting me*, and then noticed the Garnet stone glowing again, making the Old Hag retreat. She stayed on her backside, pushing herself toward the hand.

Enzo started to moan; Jordan alerted Harley, "I need to get Enzo…," she yelled.

"Don't you dare leave that circle, Jord," Harley warned, as she scanned the room for the Hag.

A heavy wind swirled around them. Items started lifting and rotating in a peculiar movement, in the form of the number 8, "*a similar start to an Ouija board session*," Harley thought, as her and Jordan watched with astonishment.

"It's a portal, Jordan!" we have to do the spell now."

"*A what?*"

"I'll explain later," she replied, as she reached for the hand.

Just before touching it, Harley stopped herself, wiped her bangs out of her eyes, and looked through the mayhem, hoping to find something to help her pick it up.

"Here," Jordan threw the Cauldron spoon at her, hitting her wrist.

"OUCH!" Harley gasped and rapidly shook her hand until the burning faded.

"Sorry," Jordan yelled, watching her struggle.

Eventually scooping the hand into the spoon, she tossed it to Jordan, and into the pot it went. The room suddenly went quiet again; all they could hear were moans from Enzo's beaten body.

The temperature dropped, sending shivers up her neck; Harley looked around and then down. Jordan nervously pushed herself closer to Harley's leg, nudging it hard, sending a violent tremble up to her hip.

"I need to see the Old Hag, Jord," she whispered.

"I saw a Ouija board near the sink, when we came in, Jordan replied, before they heard another moan from Enzo.

He tried moving, but Jordan assumed the sinister Witch wouldn't let him. They could hear hackling and laughing, through the chaos. Harley made a run for the counter, rummaging and throwing things until she found the used planchette. Firmly gripping it, she hurried back to the circle, and then the dark mist started floating in from the broken window.

Feeling another brush of wind over her back, Harley cringed. This time, the Old Hags squeal echoed loudly throughout the Cabin. Jordan cupped her ears while Enzo could only moan.

As Harley put the planchette to her eye, and looked into the direction of the smog hovering in the corner of the room. The Hag's ugly face slowly emerged from her gloomy realm and began gliding toward her. Dropping the board piece, she grasped her necklace tightly, ripping it off. She faced it toward the Old Hag, and let it dangle from her hand.

A wave of doom emanated from the eerie mist as Harley watched the malevolent force anger more, drifting rapidly from one area of the room to the next. A jolt of adrenaline surged through her body, now pushing against the old evil energy.

Harley moved towards Enzo with every ounce of strength until she was able to grab the hood of his sweater. Adrenaline now soaring, not caring if she choked him; she dragged him back into the circle where they all finally sat.

"Pass me the reversal curse, Jord," she demanded. "*DAMN, YOU, WITCH*!!!" she yelled, her face turning red with flaring anger. Starting to feel Tess's blood run through her own veins now, Harley stood strong, as she watched it`s face receded once again.

 Jordan's eyes bulged when she saw the mist drifting closer, as Harley provoked it, her fear intensifying,

"Why am I seeing it, Harley?", I don't want to die," she whispered.

"You can`t harm us," Harley screamed, ignoring Jordan's cries. She continued to ghost bate the thing, "come get me."

 The Witch finally appeared to all, and drew closer to the circle.

Jordan covered her head, afraid to see the face that she dreaded, the mist was enough.

 "No time to be scared now, Jord; it's time to end this," Harley hollered. "Your safe as long as you stay in the circle and I have the garnet."

"Did the curse say anything about sitting or standing?" Jordan asked, foolishly.

"Stay as you are," Harley replied.

Harley grabbed a spoon, dipped it into the cauldron, and passed it to Jordan.

Hesitating and clenching her eyes tight for a minute, Jordan grabbed the spoon and took her drink, allowing the warm, metallic-tasting liquid to linger momentarily. Almost throwing up, she cupped her mouth, swallowing hard.

Harley watched the stream from Jordan's eyes.

"What about Enzo?" Jordan asked as she wiped her mouth.

"I'll pour it down his throat," Harley blurted desperately.

"You wouldn`t dare, he might choke," Jordan pleaded.

"Fine, I'll try to wake him again."

Just as Harley started to push on Enzo's shoulder, objects began to fly at them; Jordan immediately dropped her chin to the floor; Harley dodged a few objects and joined.

"I think she likes him," whispered Jordan; "whenever you go near him, Harley, she freaks out."

Ignoring Jordan, she kneeled up quickly, dipping the ladle again.

Jordan watched in disbelief,

"You lied to me."

"I have no choice, Jord; he won't wake up; she paralyzed him; if I don't do this, he might die anyway. Either chokes a bit or she has her way with him. What would you rather?" Harley asked, her voice firm.

Jordan blinked, stunned at her ultimatum.

"I don't know how long the necklace will protect us from the hands of that wretched thing, Harley replied, as she held the spoon above Enzo's lips.

"Fine," Jordan cupped her ears, I don't like him that much anyway, she lied. Don't blame me if he chokes Harley."

Without another word, Harley poured the warm liquid into Enzo's mouth, and he started gagging and then coughing before he spoke,

"What the hell?" he asked, drowsily, rolling to his side, spitting, and wiping his mouth.

Harley ignored him, dumping the ladle into the cauldron one last time. She glared angrily at the Old Hag,

"This is for Tess," she said, before sucking back the fluid, quickly.

A suffocating lump formed in her throat as she choked down the taste. She grabbed the paper from her sweater pocket; looking at the sheet, while mingled sounds of screams, cries, and evil laughter filled the room; she could feel the air growing heavier as the wind picked up after the few minutes of calm.

Knowing the portal wouldn't stay open much longer, Harley ignored the chaos and quickly grabbed Enzo and Jordan's hands tightly.

"WITCH, IT ENDS NOW," she yelled. *"I DARED TO ENTER YOUR DEN! COME GET ME, IF YOU THINK YOU CAN."* I'M RIGHT HERE."

Now lowering her voice, Harley continued.

"Philomena Burton was my grandmother. You killed her, and you killed Tess; now you want me, well come on, Hag,"

"You will harm us no more; be gone; I will send you back to the grave that you belong; your curse has no more power over my family!"

And with that said, she squeezed her friend's hands tighter, and started chanting the reversal spell 13 times, the number of the Witch.

Vete, bruja, a tu reino maligno, para no volver jamás. Aqui no tens poder

The room started to slow, and the floating objects began to converge, making the Realm feel smaller and more confined. With a thunderous bang, the back door slammed shut, followed by a blinding flash of light sealing the portal.

Harley's shoulders slouched in relief and she hoped it was sealed for good. Exhausted, she dropped her head, releasing a deep sigh, letting her hands fall to her sides. Everything felt weightless; the air was still.

"Thank goodness, its over," Jordan spoke up, her voice low as she placed her trembling hand over her chest.

But just as Harley was about to reply, a powerful grip of the back of her hair, yanked her upward.

Enzo, briskly shook off his daze, swiftly grabbed Harley's ankle and pulled her back down, determined to keep her safe.

Struggling, he yelled,

"IT'S TO STRONG."

Harley dangled, painfully and helplessly in the air, by her hair and within seconds, more fear consumed her as she plummeted to the ground with a bone-jarring thud, toppling the pot and a log, sending flames roaring into a chaotic blaze.

Enzo rushed to her side, gently tapping her lifeless body, while Jordan watched, wide-eyed and terrified.

"Harley," he urged softly while shaking her, his voice laced with desperation. He scooped her up, cradling her fragile form in his arms, ready to fight against the raging fire for their survival.

Jordan continued to sit dazed, useless as every one of her muscles were constricted by terror.

"LET'S GO! Jordan, Enzo yelled, looking back, startling her, as he carried Harley to the front door.

A jolt of adrenaline, along with the scorching flames, snapped Jordan out of her zombie-like state and she followed behind quickly.

Moving as fast as they could, far away from the burning Den, they neared the mouth of the forest. Enzo gently laid Harley's limb body on the ground, and Jordan fell to her knees next to her, placing her hands on Harley's cold cheeks, shaking her, crying. But as silence stared back at her, Jordan started yelling.

"WAKE UP!"

 Seemingly hopeless, Enzo got up, turned, and walked to a tree, ran his fingers through his bangs, and gave one hard blow with his fists to the big oak that stood before him. Jordan sank deeper into the gravel and screamed, so loud, it sent echoes sailing through the deep, smoky forest.

As Enzo and Jordan sat a few feet apart, hearts heavy with the fear of losing their best friend, Harley suddenly gasped for a breath. She opened one eye, then the other, and focused on the coal-smudged face of Enzo as he rushed to her side, gripping her hand tightly.

Harley quickly became aware of the position of his other hand, resting in an inappropriate place on her chest, she swatted it away instinctively.

"Is it over?" she asked, her voice tinged with raspiness, the weight of the moment settling on her like a fog.

"Yes, I think so," Jordan smiled, and wiped her tear-stained face.

Harley could see the relief in her friends as they both helped her to her feet and said,

"Let's get out of this wicked area and agree to never return."

Relieved everyone was safe, Harley replied,

"I'm fine, Enzo, help Jordan, she's still limping."

Jordan turned back, "Hey, I'm proud of you, Harley."

"For what? she asked.

"You actually spoke Spanish on your own."

"Ya, you`ve been hiding your talents," Enzo joked, with a wink.

As they started to exit the mouth of the forest, a lady stood there. Harley looked at her, and a tear fell from her eye.

"It's the librarian," Jordan said, surprised.

"No," Harley interjected, "she`s my mother, and then ran to her.

Looking at Mary for only a moment, she hugged her tightly.

"I love you," Mary said, squeezing her. "I was so scared, Harley, but you were the only one who could end this; it's finally over."

After calming down a bit, Harley asked Mary specific question,

"By the way, do you speak Spanish? And the reason I ask you Mary, is because, when I glanced at the English reversal spell you included in the envelope, to my surprise, I started reciting something in Spanish."

"Ah, that's simple; you already knew it," Mary replied and sighed, repeating the reversal curse. "*Vete, bruja, a tu reino maligno, para no volver jamás. Aquí no tienes poder.*

"The english version..., *Be gone, witch, to your evil realm, never to return again. You have no power here.*"

"I'm confused," Harley said.

"Mary lowered her head and spoke.

"I repeatedly recited that to you when you were a baby until..."

Harley interrupted Mary's emotional words with a tight hug,

"It's done, that wicked old crone is gone. At least, I believe she's gone. At first, I wasn't really sure because, I was attacked one last time, However, I believe the portal was closed," "Harley said, with a degree of uncertainty.

Mary squeezed her eyes shut, concerned, but remained silent and hugged Harley tightly.

Harley popped her head out from Mary's grip. Looking up at her, she asked another question,

"Did you leave the letter in my parent's basement, signed M. Burton?"

"Yes, it was sent with some of your things," Mary replied.

"Who was the portrait of in the library attic?" Harley asked, starting her own interrogation now.

"That picture was of your great-great grandmother, Isabelle." Mary lowered her head, and a tear dropped. "When my mother, Philomena Burton tried to summon her from beyond the grave, the evil came through, otherwise known as the Old Hag, and killed my mother. It's a grave mistake; to meddle with the unseen and perform a ritual wrong. Promise me, Harley, never dabble in that darkness," Mary pleaded.

"Believe me, I've had enough," Harley reassured her.

"I'm just thankful the mortician was able to sew my mother's mutilated body so well, that she actually looked human again. Harley, that Witch was not merciful, she was very smart. She used my great-grandmother's portrait, along with anything else to get to you."

Harley shook her head, agreeing, and then asked her final question,

"Do you happen to know who the old graveyard keeper was?"

Mary silenced with a degree of hesitation, before explaining,

"He was your grandfather, Harley, an alcoholic, and it's a tragedy. After the death of my mother, he spiraled into bitterness. It's been years since I last spoke to him. Our cabin, once a cherished haven, became a haunting place, now known as the Old Hags Den.

Harley shivered as Mary gently wiped a tear away and continued with her story,

"I have such fond memories of my childhood there, but my father's drinking escalated, and he moved us closer to the graveyard. I eventually had to leave. That cabin became a terrifying ground for evil, over the years, many bodies were found in the area. The Old Hag claimed the lives of anyone who dared to enter."

Harley trembled at the thought, before asking another question,

"What was his name?" feeling a squeeze around her heart.

"Barnabas Burton."

Harley lowered her head, remembering his expression, just before his untimely death.

"I think he killed Tess, she whispered. He was possessed by that thing."

"Very likely," Mary said, and wrapped her arm firmly around Harley's shoulders.

"One last question," Harley looked at Mary, "do we happen to have any witch lineage in our family?"

"Ah…," Mary winked, "that's a whole other story, for another time."

As Harley and Mary walked ahead silently, the faint sounds of Enzo and Jordan's bickering drifted from behind, adding a lively backdrop to the end of their morbid ordeal.

Or, was it really the end?

9 781806 234189